The Penny Predicament

The Penny Predicament

A Coin Chronicles Novel

By Veola Vazquez, Ph.D.

Illustrated by Lauren Boebinger Lewis

Copyright © 2016 Veola Vazquez, Ph.D.

Illustrations and cover design copyright © 2016 Lauren Boebinger Lewis

Double Letter Press

ISBN: 0692394907
ISBN-13: 978-0-692-39490-8

Printed in the United States of America

Visit www.VeolaVazquez.com

For my boys

Chapter 1
No New Jersey

"**L**AID OFF."

I've got my ear to my parents' door and it's those two words I hear mixed with the clomping noise of my dad's boots on the wood floor.

I shake my head and whisper them to myself over and over again. "Laid off … laid off … laid off." They start to sound like a foreign language after I say them too many times. But I know what they mean. They mean that Dad no longer has a J-O-B.

Nope, "laid off" is not the news I expected when Dad came in the house after work today and asked Mom to follow him to their room. When I decided to eavesdrop, I guess I expected something other than …

Laid off
Jobless
Without work.

It's this news that's causing my heart to beat and a line of sweat to mount on my brow. I grit my teeth and inch even closer to their door. My only prayer is that I can listen in without my own nervous breathing giving me away.

Lucky for me, Mom's voice grows louder and drowns out some of my noise. "Dex, are you telling me that they laid you off without even two weeks' pay?"

Dad lets out a big sigh. "Sharon, I told you. It's

the same for all of us. They let five of us go today."

Dad's shoes make that clomping sound again, closer to the door and then farther away. Back and forth, back and forth. With each step nearer the door, I feel a jolt of fear that he might find me.

Knowing that eavesdropping is considered a major crime in my house doesn't matter. I have to hear more, so I stay, biting my lip in anticipation.

When his boots grow silent, I suck in a breath and hold it, trying to keep as quiet as I can. Even with my adrenaline pumping, and sweat starting to pour down my face,

I can't pull myself away.

"That's not right! How could they do that?" Although I can still hear her, mom's voice is quieter now and trembling. She sounds like she's about to cry.

I can understand why.

Laid off is what happened to Mike Winters' dad last year and he ended up in New Jersey–of all places!

I'm a California guy myself. San Francisco is my life and the thought of moving to one of the smallest states in the country is not my idea of a good time, especially after I heard that Mike Winters has to endure 20 degree temperatures for months on end.

Needing to know if Jersey might be my fate, I press my ear closer to the door and do my best to stop breathing.

After a few seconds, I can't hold my breath any longer and have to let it out. I press my lips together and try to force the air through the tiny hole without making noise. Instead of silence, what comes out is an unexpected chirpy little whistle that, for some reason, makes me chuckle.

I hear footsteps coming swiftly toward the door and it's clear that I've been caught.

I freeze.

I suddenly feel like Luke Skywalker when he faced Darth Vader on the Death Star. I have no place to hide and my father is probably going to kill me. At least if I had a lightsaber I might not have to think of a good excuse for spying.

Without any kind of real explanation for my presence, I drop to the ground and pretend to look for something. As I move my hands across the floor in search of the mystery object, I hear a creak in the wood and see the tips of Dad's boots. I look up and give him my biggest grin.

"Jake, what are you doing out here?" He clenches his jaw and frowns.

"Uh, I dropped my ..." Think of something, Jake! Think! "I dropped a coin."

There's a long silence while Dad stares down at me.

"Uh, one of my collectible coins. It rolled down the hall. I think it stopped somewhere around here."

I continue feeling around the floor even though I

know that it's not a good idea to lie to Dad.

"Get in here." Dad motions into his room. His voice sounds tight so I brace myself for punishment. He's told me about 321 times not to listen in on their conversations.

Yes, I admit it. I've done it before. But, I had a good reason every time. Unfortunately, I was caught the last time and ended up with a two week ban from video games.

I take slow steps into their room, feeling like a dog caught eating off the kitchen table. Mom sits on the bed with her legs crossed tight and her arms folded up against her chest. Her brown curls fall down over her eyes and I can tell that she's not in the mood for games.

I choose a safe spot a distance away from her on the bed; but she gets up and stands next to Dad so that they are now both staring down at me.

By the looks on their faces, my punishment will definitely be worse this time.

Why do I do this to myself?

"First of all, we know you were listening," Dad says.

"But –"

"Don't try to make excuses." A big frown curves across Mom's lips making her appear older. Her pale skin looks clammy and despite her eyes being dry, I can tell she's on the

verge of tears.

I lower my head and let out a sigh. "Yeah, I was listening."

Dad clears his throat. "You'll need to go to your room while we think of your punishment."

I stand to leave, glad that I won't have to endure their stares any longer; but my stomach flips a little at the thought that they have to talk about my punishment. It's always worse when they take time to think about it.

I move toward the door with my head down, trying not to imagine all the possible consequences of my actions.

"Wait," says Dad.

I make a slow turn.

He looks at Mom and she gives him a nod. "We need to

tell you something."

There's a moment of quiet.

"If you don't already know, I got laid off today, Jake."

I clear the bubble growing in my throat. "Uh, what are you going to do?"

Dad exchanges a quick glance with Mom. She lowers her eyes. "We're not sure yet. But, I need to find work soon."

My first thought is of Mike Winters. "Does this mean we have to move?"

Mom's head jerks up. It's a long few seconds before Dad responds. "We can't promise anything,

Jake. We just need to pray." Dad takes another look at Mom and she nods. "Now go to your room and think about what you've done. We'll talk to you about it later."

With an even bigger feeling of dread than when I started eavesdropping, I walk to my room and plop down on my bed. I tug at the edges of my *Star Wars* comforter while I stare at the wall with the idea that I'm supposed to

The only thing I can think about though is Dad's news. I listen to the sound of my own voice while using those two words again. "Laid off," with an Australian accent. "Laid off," like a Texan. And "Laid off," like an Englishman.

No matter how I say it, it still gives me a dry mouth, a quickened heartbeat and images of trudging through the snow to get to school.

When I tire of listening to the round-the-world tour of those two words, I roll off the bed and onto the floor. I lean back expecting to lounge on the throw rug. Instead, I find a carpet of coins and hit my head on a forgotten stack of quarters. Not completely surprised, I groan and massage the pain away.

As the ache begins to fade, I pick up a penny and rub it on my sleeve. Staring at the ceiling, my mind goes back to images of New Jersey.

I can see it all. I'm in school and Mike and I are the only students. He's wearing a parka the size of a grizzly bear and I'm shirtless and shivering.

I shudder at the thought. That can't be my future!

I shoot up into a sitting position and look around my room. Everything I know is here in San Francisco. "Laid off" could mean the end of everything!

Between thoughts of moving and knowing that I also have a consequence coming, my entire body starts to jitter. Needing to keep my mind and my hands busy, I shine a few more old coins while I wait to find out how long I'll be grounded.

I look around my room and see evidence of my growing coin collection. Old coins, new coins, collectibles. They're everywhere. And they're my prize possessions. At least if I have to move, I'd have my collection to keep me company.

Just as I'm about to shine a few collectible quarters, I hear a tap on my door. I jump up, thinking my jail sentence is over. But the door cracks open and it's just my 9-year-old brother, Alex.

"Hey, Jake."

I plop back down in the middle of my coins. "You better not come in here. Mom and Dad will get you too." I run my hand over a stack of nickels, feeling the cool metal against my skin.

He whispers,

"Are you in trouble?"

His green eyes widen but a little smirk teases at his lips.

"I guess." I jump back onto my bed and slide my hands behind my head, trying not to look concerned. "But don't worry, I'll be out of here in no time."

"Well, I just beat your high score on bowling." Alex laughs. "Just wondering when you want to challenge me."

His squeaky giggle makes me grit my teeth. It's made worse by the fact that I probably won't be playing bowling or any other video game for a while.

I'm about to tell him what he can do with that bowling game, but he closes the door before I can say a thing. I hear him laughing all the way down the hall.

With Alex gone, I make a loud grunt hoping to ease the knot growing in my stomach and then go back to my accents. "Laid off," I yell with a cowboy twang and my door flies open.

I jump off my bed, ready to make sure Alex never comes back again.

But it isn't Alex.

Dad stands in the doorway stone-faced and with his arms folded across his chest. Because of my big leap off the bed and the fact that I'm wearing socks on the wood floor, I slide straight for him and I can't stop. I land right at his feet. His jaw tightens as he stares down at me just like he did earlier. His voice is cold. "Are you ready for your

Chapter 2
Crazy Consequences

Eavesdropping isn't worth it. I'm three and a half weeks into my punishment and I regret every second I spent outside my parents' door the day they got the news of Dad's layoff.

If I thought my last punishment for listening in on my parents was bad, this time it's been total agony.

One month of no video games!

And every time that I've walked by Alex with a video game controller in his hand, it's left me dry-mouthed and shaky. Watching him makes me want to grab the controller and bury it in the backyard.

It's that temptation that's eating at me as I stare at the screen watching him beat his high score in bowling again. Crazy-angry tension has my shoulders all knotted up and I feel like I'm about to explode.

"You should probably go in the other room," Alex says. "I can tell that this is hard for you."

Despite the sincere sounding words, Alex's goofy smile gives away his attempt at mocking me. I take a step toward him with my fists balled.

I don't even notice when Mom enters the room until she waves a hand in front of my face. "I'm going grocery shopping. I need you to come and help me."

"Huh?"

"Shopping. Grab your shoes."

I take another peek at Alex and he's staring at me with that cheesy grin again. "You have to go shopping, Jake. No time for bowling." He says it with that sing-song voice that grates on my nerves.

With as much self-control as I can muster, I tell myself to ignore him and then go to my room. I pull my shoes on in record time, with a voice inside me telling me that if I don't get out of the house, I might have to do something to wipe that grin off Alex's face.

Like I said, eavesdropping isn't worth it.

Once we get to the store, I push the grocery cart, trailing behind Mom. It's loaded down with food and one wheel is frozen in place.

"Pick up the pace," Mom says. She takes a quick glance back at me and frowns.

I want to say, I NEVER ASKED TO COME TO THE GROCERY STORE! I never asked to strain my back and feel my muscles burn! But that wouldn't go over well. Keeping track of the cost of food while grocery shopping is part of my punishment.

Mom throws a loaf of bread into the cart and I stop with a jerk. While she checks the contents of the basket, I fish in my pocket for a pen and add the price of the bread to our list. I do a bit of quick addition and update the running total.

"$150.21," I tell her.

She frowns and looks at the floor. "We still need mayo and lunch meat ..." Her voice trails off and she stares off into space for a moment. "Things are going to be tight."

This isn't the first time I've heard those words recently.

Ever since Dad's layoff, Mom's become obsessed with tracking every dollar spent on food. And we're always

"going to be tight"

I gulp at the thought of what could become of our family if Dad doesn't find a job soon. I never realized how much food cost!

I follow Mom through the rest of the store, the pain in my arms growing as I push the handicapped basket and watch our grocery total rise. When we finally leave the store, my aches and pains are forgotten when I spy the glint of a coin between a wall near the exit and a vending machine.

I park the basket and peer into the space. A scuffed-up quarter sits lodged between the machine and the wall.

My first thought? It would all be worth it–the basket, my tired arms, my aching legs–if I could get my hands on that coin.

I take a quick glance around. Crowds of people

funnel in and out of the store. Hoping they won't run me over and Mom won't mind my temporary stop, I crouch on my hands and knees and reach behind the machine.

I feel for the coin and my finger barely grazes it, so I push my body as far into the area between the wall and the machine as I can. With one last reach, I wrap my hand around the quarter and feel the squish of something sticky.

"Jacob Samuel King!" The angry tone of Mom's voice jolts me. "Get out of there!" She yanks on my sleeve and tries to pull me to a stand but I can't get my arm to budge. Mom yanks harder, but the harder she pulls, the harder it is to move my arm. I wiggle it and try sliding it up and down but my sleeve must be stuck on something.

I look back at her and shrug. When she tightens

her jaw I take a breath and try again with all my strength. I pull and hear a … zzzzrrrrrichhhhhh!

With that screechy sound, my sleeve comes loose and I fly out of the hole, sliding across the floor and right into a gray-haired granny.

From my place on the floor, I watch the old lady teeter-totter and pray she won't fall on me.

"Oh, uh, no …" Granny's last words sound like my screams on a rollercoaster last summer.

But when she falls, I don't think she enjoys the ride.

Neither do I.

Granny lands right on my stomach and knocks the wind out of me. Her face twists in shock and she blasts me with words I never thought a grandma could say. She finishes it off with, "You little devil! Where's your mother?"

Thinking I might look more innocent in a ball on the floor, I stay there and point to Mom. The shock on her face almost matches Granny's. She pushes our basket aside and whisks Granny off the floor. She dusts her off and gives her a string of, "I'm so sorry. Please forgive us. Accept our apologies. I can't say how sorry we are."

As she rattles off the "I'm sorries," I hear the familiar trill of Mom's cell phone chiming Dad's ringtone. She takes a quick look at her purse but doesn't answer it.

Granny straightens her shower curtain-like dress, squints her eyes at me and turns back to Mom. "You should do something about that child. He's out of control."

Mom gives me an angry look and then puts on a fake smile. "Of course, I'm so sorry, ma'am. I'll have a good talk with him."

At this point, I'm still on the ground. I don't want to risk getting up and looking too big to be getting into that kind of trouble. According to Mom, 12-year-olds "should have better manners."

"Get up, Jake." Mom's voice is gritty.

That dirt-in-the-throat sound in her voice has become a little too familiar lately. Not wanting to risk making things worse, I jump up and stand straight as a board, trying to look respectable.

"Apologize to the lady, Jake."

I notice the people passing by on either side of us are starting to stare. "Please forgive me, ma'am," I say in my most grown-up voice. "I won't ever do that again."

Granny's lips are little lines. She stares at me. "Do you promise, young man?"

"Uh, yes. I promise," I say, crossing my fingers behind my back.

"Then shake on it," Granny holds out her hand.

Without thinking, I put out mine too, forgetting that I'm still holding the quarter. Just as I'm about to slide my hand into Granny's I catch myself and move the coin into my other fist. I shake with her thinking I've finally fixed things. I realize that's a mistake when she yanks her hand away.

She lets out a squeaky, "Ewwww!" and stares down at her palm.

I look down at mine too.

Both our hands are covered in pink gum!

It hits me. That's why the quarter was sticky.

Granny's hand starts to tremble and she makes a low growling kind of noise. I look to Mom but she's frozen now, watching us like a horror movie.

"I …" I want to make it all better. But no words come.

Finally, Granny curls up her lips and stalks out of

the store.

I come to my senses as I realize that the grocery traffic is still moving around us.

"Oops!"

I give Mom my best …

"I didn't mean it" shrug.

She takes a moment, swallows hard and then speaks. "That coin better be worth it," she says. She motions for me to grab the basket and stomps out of the store.

Worth it? I lift my chin and push my shoulders back. I'd definitely hunt down that coin again. Actually, I'd go after any coin, even a penny.

I push the basket with all the strength I have left and run to catch up with Mom. Her jaw is clenched like stone. A breeze bounces her curls and she pushes them out of her face with a jerky movement. "Put the bags in the trunk," she says as she sits in the car.

Before I start loading the groceries, I pull the quarter out of my pocket. In all the chaos with Granny, I still hadn't had a chance to look at it.

I check the front of the coin and a ripple of excitement runs through me. It's an Oklahoma 2008 quarter. My state quarter collection is almost complete. I rub the little "P" printed on the front, thankful that I found one that was made in Pennsylvania and glad that I didn't get another "D" coin, minted in Denver.

I turn it over to admire the back. It's still camouflaged by gum. I stick my thumb in my mouth to get a little spit, wipe it off as much as I can and then clean it with my T-shirt.

When it's a bit shinier, I attempt to slide it back into my pocket. Just as I do, mom starts the car and blasts the horn, making me jump. The coin fumbles out of my hand and rolls toward the back tire. I take a quick glance up and find Mom staring at me through the side-view mirror with angry eyes.

I grab the coin off the ground and then peek into the side mirror to see if she's still watching; but she's on the phone and no longer keeping an eye on me. I stuff the coin back in my pocket and load the bags into the trunk.

When I finally hop into the front seat, she still has her cell phone to her ear.

"No. You're kidding me." She covers her mouth then smacks the steering wheel.

I shrug my hands into the air to ask, "What's up?"

She turns away and breathes deep. "Okay, I'll talk to you when you get home. Love you." She clicks off the phone and we sit in silence for a long few minutes.

Finally, I try to nudge some information out of her. "So …"

She grips the steering wheel and leans her head on it, not saying a word. After we've been sitting in silence for longer than just a few minutes, my stomach begins to knot up. My fingers do a little dance on the door while my leg jitters.

I sit in constant motion, studying two birds as they peck at something on the concrete outside. Just as my frantic movement and bird watching starts to help my stomach loosen, mom grabs my arm.

She jabs a finger close to my face.

"Stop!"

The yell-whisper and the anger in her eyes give me a jolt. I send my hands to my lap and try to calm my leg. Even the birds must have been spooked by Mom because they're nowhere to be found.

Within seconds, Mom lowers her head into her hands. "I'm sorry, Jake." She lets out a loud blast of air and turns toward me. "It's just that …" She looks at the ceiling of the car, as if she can find the rest of what she wants to say written there. "Your dad just got three job rejection letters."

I search the ceiling, too, because I don't know how to respond. "Uh, sorry Mom."

A tear rolls down her cheek. "I just don't know

how we're going to make it. These groceries alone cost a fortune."

I put my hand on Mom's shoulder and don't say a word. It takes all the energy I have to stay quiet.

But my mind won't stop running.

Almost a month already and Dad still doesn't have a job. I don't know much about jobs and interviews and stuff, but that can't be good.

Just as I start to sweat at the thought of moving to New Jersey, I have an idea.

If money is going to be a problem, I'll have to

do something about it.

Chapter 3
Pancakes and Plans

My wiener dog, Wally, wakes me up the next morning licking my face, leaving saliva on my chin. When I finally push him to the end of the bed and wipe myself off, I remember my dream.

I was standing by a swimming pool as giant gold coins fell from the sky, filling the pool. When one of them almost hit me on the head, I ducked under an awning and took a look up to the sky. There were no clouds and no sun, just gold everywhere.

The waves of gold in the pool sparkled in the sun, blinding me for a moment; but I jumped, landed right in the middle of the pool and started swimming.

What a dream! I pull my blanket tight around me and roll over. If only the dream had been real. Swimming in gold! Yep, that's all I'd need to solve my family's problems.

The possibility of Dad never finding a job makes both my head and my heart hurt. And after seeing the way Mom acted in the car yesterday, thoughts of it kept me awake half the night. But by the time I fell asleep, I had come up with a plan to help.

And it would start today!

I count to three and hop out of bed, stumbling to the closet. Wally nips at my heels and I try to push him away, but he keeps coming back.

Now I regret my crazy younger years when I taught him to chase me and eat sausages from between my toes. He hasn't forgotten–and my toes have seen better days.

But battling Wally as I get dressed wakes me up and gives me the energy I need. By the time I pull a sweater over my head and take off to the bathroom, I'm ready to launch my plan into action.

As I stand in front of the bathroom mirror, I try to slick down my bumpy curls with a little water.

Mom's dark waves and pale skin combined with

Dad's tight ringlets and chocolate tone have given me a mixture of curly brown hair and tan coloring. But sometimes those curls don't cooperate. This is one of those days, so I give up and put on a hat.

Thinking of my plan, I walk to the kitchen with a bounce in my step. I smell the syrup before I even get there. Pancakes! The perfect beginning to a cool San Francisco Saturday morning.

When I enter the kitchen, I find the entire family is already up and busy.

"Morning, Mom."

She looks up from the griddle with half a smile. Her eyes look red and she doesn't say anything. I take a quick mood check of Alex and Dad.

Alex has his fork to his mouth, stuffing an entire pancake in–

Dad sits in his usual spot in the living room–a brown recliner–with his laptop. He doesn't take his eyes off the screen. I peer over and catch a glimpse of a job hunt website. I shake his shoulder to get his attention.

"Hey, Dad, what's up?"

He closes the computer and sets it aside. "Hey, son." He puts his arms out to give me a hug and I throw myself at him with a bit more force than I planned.

He grunts, "Ugh."

I pull away, avoiding eye contact. Alex raises his eyebrows and wags his finger at me. I poke him in the ribs, hoping it will make him keep quiet, but instead it makes him laugh and

Spit out his milk.

He gets up to come after me, but Dad clears his throat loudly. It makes Alex sit back down and I fill my mouth with food. "Saw-wey, Dad," I say through my pancakes as I sit too.

"First of all, no more tackles. If you can't give a hug, we'll just stick with high-fives. Alright?"

"Sure, Dad." I take a swig of milk. "So what's going on today?"

He rubs his belly a bit and leans back in his chair. "Well, your Mom talked to you, right? About the job search?"

My heart beats a little bit faster. "Uh, yeah." I dig back into my food and don't look up.

Dad gets up from the recliner and sits next to me at the table. "I don't want you guys to worry about it, okay?" He pats both Alex and me on the back.

"You'll get another job, Dad. I'm not worried about it," Alex says through his pancakes.

I pick up my milk again and it jostles back and forth in the glass as my hand shakes. I put it down without taking a drink.

"No big deal, Dad." I pause to gather my nerve to ask what's really on my mind. I have to find out if my plan is still necessary. "Um … I'm still just wondering if we might have to move."

Alex clunks his fork on his plate. "Who said we're

moving?"

"Nobody has said anything about moving." Dad leans forward and pats my back again. "Just pray Jake, and let us worry about that."

When my leg joins the shaking party, the only prayer I can muster is for Dad to leave me alone. Plan or no plan, thinking about the whole thing makes me

Dad stares at me for a minute with that "poor kid" look. I try to stop the leg movement by biting my lip but the other leg joins in. When the table starts to look like the victim of an earthquake, I think Dad gets the hint that I don't want to talk anymore and goes back to his chair.

I take that as my chance to get out. I dump my dishes in the sink and go back to my room.

I chuck my hat onto my bed. What's my problem? Between the wobbly hands and shaky legs, I can't even trust my own body to behave anymore.

I sit feeling sorry for myself for a few moments but come to the decision that I need to put my plan into action. I grab my cell phone off the desk and close my bedroom door.

I find my best friend, Ben, in my favorite contacts and sit down in front of my closet. I cringe at the boxes piled high with my old toys. For months Mom has been telling me to get rid of them. It would take a while to go through them now, but I'm grateful to have the old junk.

Ben answers.

"Hey. I need your help."

"Sure. What's up?"

"Uh … I need to make some money fast. And I have an idea. But I can't do it alone."

"Money? Um … okaaaay …" Ben's voice trails off. I can hear his doubt already.

I dump the contents of a box onto the ground in front of me. "Listen. I know I've had some crazy ideas before, but you've gotta trust me."

Maybe I shouldn't have used the words "trust me" with Ben. The last time I told him that, we ended up almost getting lost in San Francisco.

"What?" I hear the noise of the phone moving around on Ben's end. "Sorry, I had to clean out my ears. Did you just ask me to trust you?"

I push some old Legos and action figures into a

pile. "Yeah, just listen. I need to sell some stuff. And it has to be done today. We have to do a yard sale at your house."

"A yard sale?" Ben pauses. "What kind of stuff?" There's a change in his voice. I think I have his attention.

I look at my pile and start counting. "So far I have about 10 old Nintendo games, a Gameboy, a huge pile of Legos, and about 15 action figures."

"And you think you're going to make some money with that? Who are you planning on selling it to, a bunch of 6 year olds?" Ben laughs.

"Well, what do you think I should do, sell my shoes or something?" I grab one of my Nikes and toss it into the basketball net on the back of my door.

Yes, three points!

Trying to ignore the black marks it leaves on the door, I close my eyes as it bumps to the floor.

"Dude, and maybe your clothes and TV, too," Ben says.

I stare at my new 20 inch flat screen. Mom and Dad bought it for my birthday just a few months ago after he got the job that just laid him off. I got my cell phone at the same time. Ben was right. The TV alone could bring a good $150.

What else could I sell? I scratch my head and look around my room at all the stuff that's worth money. My San Francisco Giants jersey, a signed baseball, a pile of DVDs under my TV—any of it could bring in some cash.

I study every inch of my room. Distracted by my thoughts, I don't notice Wally jump up. Before I can do anything, he gets me right in the eye with that long tongue of his. Holding him over my head with one arm, I stare him down. "You could bring me at least $200."

I think I hear Wally whimper at that comment.

"So?" Ben says.

"Let me look through my stuff and I'll bring it over to your house in an hour."

I check my watch. I have until 9 a.m. With Ben's house being located on the corner of a busy street, it's the perfect location for a yard sale. We wouldn't even need signs. All I'd need to do is provide plenty of reasons to stop.

I toss the phone onto my bed, plop down next to it and scan my room again. I stare at the TV. I probably shouldn't sell it–at least not yet.

When my eyes land on my coin jars, things become clearer. My collection has to be worth something.

Maybe even a lot.

Chapter 4
Bicycle Bomb

I find two large backpacks in the garage and fill them with goodies for the sale. When they're bulging with stuff, I throw one over each shoulder and hope Mom and Dad won't ask what's in them.

I find Dad in the living room sitting in his recliner. "I'm going to Ben's for a while. Okay?"

He peers at me over his laptop. His eyebrows narrow as he looks back and forth between the two bags. "You planning to stay a while?"

"Ha!" I laugh. "Right. Funny, Dad."

We stare at each other for a long minute. I gulp and wonder whether I should come up with an excuse. Nothing comes to mind.

Dad closes the laptop a bit and shakes his head. "You boys. Always up to something."

I fidget under his gaze, moving my weight from one foot to the other.

Finally, he waves me off. "Be back by dinner time."

I run to the garage to get my bike, not waiting around for him to change his mind.

I pull the first backpack over both shoulders and loosen the straps on the second, making them long enough to fit on top of the first. I pull it on and hop on my bike. Pushing the handheld clicker to raise the garage door, I start pedaling toward the opening.

Sunlight beams in as the door rises and suddenly I'm blind. I keep moving anyway, hoping I don't run into anything.

There's no time to waste.

But then I hear the clatter of Wally's claws on the concrete behind me, letting me know that I forgot to lock his doggie door.

I turn to look at him but black and blue spots block my vision. Even though I can't see him, I can still hear him. I try to keep him in the garage with a growl and a "Stay!" as I exit.

I hit the clicker to close the door behind me but just as it starts to lower, the sound of his claws grows louder and faster in my direction. Images of a 12-pound wiener dog smashed under the garage door flash through my mind. I throw down my bike. I have to save him!

Everything happens in slow motion. I hear my voice in that far-away sound you hear in movies,

I run to put my foot in front of the sensor that stops the door. But the concrete is slippery with dust and I slide to the floor with the two backpacks under me. The door stops as I hit the ground and I hear a … CRACK … from one of the packs.

To make things worse, Wally jumps on my face and licks me over and over.

Can't that dog get enough?

I push him off and get up, leaving the packs on the ground.

"When will you ever learn?" I realize I sound just like my mom, which sends a shiver down my spine.

Trying to feel more like myself and less like my mother, I give Wally a quick squeeze and then deposit him inside the house. Once I've made sure the door to the house is secure and he's not going to sneak out, I take a quick look inside both packs.

What I find not only breaks my heart but also breaks the bank. Three smashed DVDs!

That dog just cost me at least fifteen bucks.

I toss the movies in the trash and get back on my bike praying the morning will get better.

Riding downhill on the sidewalk, I start the two-block distance to Ben's house. A heavy gust of wind swirls small pieces of street trash around my tires and over my head. The cool air energizes me and I pick up speed. Barreling downhill, I have a good feeling about my upcoming yard sale. With two heavy packs full of toys and other old junk, there's no way I could finish this day with less than a few hundred dollars.

Excitement drives a tingle through my body and I suddenly feel like I can do anything. The sun is shining, the skies are blue and it's going to be my day.

I push my bike harder, faster past each house. The street is empty of cars, so I lift my front tire and make the bike sail off the sidewalk and onto the road.

"Yeah!" I yell.

When I land, I can't help but notice that I feel lighter. I take a look behind me and see a group of action figures laying on the ground and Legos scattered on the concrete.

There's been an explosion.

Backpack Number One is wounded.

I stop the bike in the middle of the street and look around me. As I bend to check the disaster, my signed Giants baseball tips out of the bag. I watch it start to roll and, for the first time, I wish that I didn't live in San Francisco, a city famous for its hills.

The ball picks up speed and flies down the slope. I panic. I can't lose that ball!

I drop my bike and Backpack Number One in the middle of the street and take off running.

I never realized how fast a baseball could move; but my legs find out. When I start wheezing and coughing, sucking in the cool morning bay air, I realize that I can't run as fast as it can roll.

I slow and watch the ball move farther and farther down the street toward a gutter. I don't want to give up, but my lungs feel like they're on fire and I have to let it go.

Dejected, I turn around and walk back up the hill, shaking my head at the realization of what I just lost.

My breath catches when I look to where I left all my stuff. A woman has stopped her car in front of my bike and has gotten out. She has her hand on her hip, pouting her red lips.

"Is this your bike?"

Even though I'm still wheezing and my legs are cramping, I run up the hill. "Uh, yeah."

Just as I get there, a truck stops behind her.

Could things get any worse?

Realizing the scene I've just caused, I throw my hand over my eyes and pray to

 **disappear.**

Chapter 5
Selling the Stuff

When I hear a car door slam, I peek through my fingers. The man from the truck is running toward me.

"Are you okay, son? Should I call an ambulance?" the Truck Man asks.

I look around. "For who?"

Truck Man surveys me from head to toe and then looks back at my bike and the scattered toys.

"were you hit?"

I look at myself from toe to head, "I don't think so. Those action figures can be pretty hard, but none of them hit me."

Truck Man scrunches his eyebrows. He looks like he's about to ask me a question.

But I've already been here too long and Ben is waiting for me. I check my watch and sprint the few feet to my mess. I sweep up the action figures but scrape my hand on the concrete and wince from the pain.

"Let me help you," Truck Man says and picks up the Legos one by one. The thought crosses my mind to leave them but Legos are expensive. I could get at least five bucks for just the pieces on the ground.

I let Truck Man finish with them while I stuff the action figures in Backpack Number Two. I give the pack a stern warning, "You better do your job," and hop back on my bike. Truck Man is nice enough to pile the Legos into the outside pocket of the pack.

I inch my bike toward the sidewalk and look up. Tight Lips Lady has gotten back in her car. She's shaking her head and tapping her steering wheel, just waiting for me to get out of the way.

When I reach the sidewalk, she creeps by me so slow I could have passed her on my bike. She gives me another head shake. I feel like returning her dirty look but instead I smile and wave.

Knowing my peak garage sale hours are running out, I take off and build up speed again. I coast to the bottom of the hill where the street dead ends. There, I find the baseball only a foot from a ditch that has the words "Drains to the Ocean" stamped in the concrete.

Thank you, God!

I hadn't expected to find it at all. But now that I see it's so close to

disappearing into eternity,

I throw the bike down again and give the ball a big kiss. If it had gone down that drain, I would have been out one-hundred bucks.

I roll the ball over in my hand, checking every stitch. The trip down the hill has taken its toll. Black scratches cover one side and the signature has a dent in it.

I grit my teeth. Not only have I lost fifteen dollars in DVDs on my way to Ben's house, but now my ball is probably worth about

twenty bucks less.

A sudden heavy breeze blows and causes my hood to flop over my head. That's all it takes to make me realize I've been standing staring at the ball way too long. I stuff it in my hoodie pocket and ride a little lopsided to Ben's house hoping it won't fall out again.

Ben's waiting outside with two card tables set up when I get there. He's sitting on the sidewalk with his long legs up on a big cardboard box that has "Yard Sale" written on it. With his driveway right in front of an intersection, nothing would block the view of what I have to offer.

At least something about this day would go my way.

"Hey, man." I high-five Ben and let both backpacks fall onto a table with a thump.

Ben gets up. He pushes his long dark hair out of his eyes and adjusts his glasses. "What do you have in there? Rocks?" He joins me at the table and peers into one of the bags as I pull on the zipper.

I look up at him but ignore his question and give him a fake smile. Number Two beckons me to unpack so I start pulling stuff out. I stack the DVDs in three piles and put the CDs next to them. I line up the action figures in a pretend battle, hoping that kids won't be able to resist.

The small front pocket of the pack holds my coins. I pull out a booklet with four state quarters minted in 2009. It's an extra set, so it won't hurt to sell it. I tilt open the cover of the booklet and set it up.

"So, how much do you think you're going to make today?" Ben picks up the coin booklet.

I cringe and snatch the booklet from him. I gently place it back in its spot. "Maybe $250. Could have been more but ..." I give a heavy sigh. "Well, it's a long story. It's been a hard morning."

"Two-hundred and fifty dollars? How are you planning to do that? Are you going to charge $5 per quarter?" Ben laughs.

I wave my arm across my treasures and smile. "DVDs, CDs, Wii games, my Giants jersey, my signed World Series ball! That's the least I can make."

"Uh, what ball?"

Ben gives me a smirk.

I smack my hand to my forehead. After all the work to get it back, how could I have forgotten? I dig in my pocket and pull it out.

Ben gives the ball a doubtful look. "Nice ball."

"Don't ask."

A grin creeps up his face. "Well, don't you at least have a stand for that thing?"

"I did." I shake away the memory. "I sat on it."

He laughs. "Why doesn't that surprise me?" Then

he thumps me on the forehead.

I put up my fists, ready for a rumble, dancing around him like a boxer.

Even though Ben's at least a foot taller than me, he doesn't hold back. He takes on his boxing stance and starts jabbing.

Knowing I can't take him, I give it my best. We move onto the grass and I throw a punch and make contact with his left arm. There isn't an ounce of strength behind it though. It's impossible to make much of an impact with arms as thin as pencils.

Ben doesn't even whimper.

Lucky for me though, his feet are still too big for his body. My little punch jostles him. He teeters a bit and then stumbles forward. I'm about to declare victory when he crashes into me and we both tumble to the ground. That doesn't stop him. He brings out his karate moves with a few air kicks and then twists my spaghetti arms behind my back.

"Give up?" Ben laughs.

"Never!"

He holds me for a few seconds but I'm unwilling to plead for mercy. Then, I hear a car door slam.

"I give up," I yell and Ben lets me jump to my feet.

My first customer has arrived. A man about as old as my grandpa has his hands on the ball. He takes off his glasses and puts it up close to his face. I stand back and let him take his time. But when he starts rubbing the scuff marks, I step up.

"Those are nothing. I'm sure they'll come off real easy," I say.

"Hmm. It's not in mint condition, is it?" Mr. Grandpa says.

"Uh." Why did that backpack have to explode? "No, it isn't. But, I'll give you a good price."

He places his glasses back on the bridge of his nose and stares at me over them. "How much do you want for it?"

Temptation sets in.

I need the money and should ask for as much as possible. But what if a high price sends the guy back to his car with nothing?

The tension in my jaw grows. I look at Ben and he

shrugs.

"How about $100 dollars," I say with a firm nod, knowing that it's probably worth closer to $80, if that.

Mr. Grandpa raises his eyebrows and laughs. I'm close enough to him that I can smell the bacon on his breath. "Wow. You're a wheeler and a dealer, aren't you?"

I take a step back, stand straighter and point at the ball. "That's a World Series ball."

He clears his throat. "It looks like it's been through a lot. How about I give you $50?"

My heart jumps.

Half price?

When I stand too long with my mouth hanging open, Ben grabs my shoulder and pulls me aside.

"You better take it. You're not going to get a better offer than that." He pauses and points back at the ball. "I mean, look at that thing."

"But, it didn't look like that this morning. It was in perfect condition just an hour ago." My voice cracks a little as the disappointment slices through my words. I look back at Mr. Grandpa. He has his eye on the jersey now.

"Well, it's not perfect anymore," Ben says. "Come on, Jake. If you want some money, sell it to him."

Mr. Grandpa picks up the jersey and turns it to look at both the front and back. If I can haggle the right price, I know I'll have him sold on it, too.

Before he can set it down, I walk back to the table and put on my salesman voice.

"How about you take both for $120?"

Mr. Grandpa squints and rubs his chin. He studies the ball and the jersey.

"How about I take both for **$100?**"

Chapter 6
Mr. Money Maker

Mr. Grandpa is better at wheeling and dealing than I am. He has me stuck. The ball and jersey should be worth so much more than $100. But I have no choice. I take a heavy breath and glance at the ground. "Okay, you've got a deal."

He folds the jersey over his arm and pulls out his wallet. "Great. My grandson will love them."

I hold out my hand and Mr. Grandpa counts out the whole $100 in $20 bills. The money is stiff as I smash it into my pocket. Feeling a bit gypped, I watch him leave with my ball and jersey in his hands and a big smile on his face.

After he leaves, things are quiet. Ben and I stand next to one of the tables but then sink onto the cement with our feet dangling off the curb while we wait for more business.

I hang my head between my knees while Ben picks at a piece of grass. He finally breaks the silence. "I don't get why you're selling your stuff. Your family is rich."

This makes me sit up straight. "What? We're not rich. How could you even say that?"

"Come on, Jake. You've got a brand new 20 inch flat screen in your room. To me, that's rich."

I nod. "I guess it seems like it, huh?"

"Then why are you selling your stuff?"

A few cars pass by slowly while their drivers gawk at my tables. But no one stops. The exhaust fumes float our way and make me cough.

Inside I argue with myself about whether I should tell Ben what's happened. I look back at the tables, then up and down the street.

Not One Customer.

"My dad got laid off," I whisper.

"What? You're mad about a day off?" he says really loud.

The fact that he's shown absolutely no tact about my situation makes me cringe. I groan and punch him in the arm. "No. My dad got laid off. Okay?" This time I say it louder to make sure he gets the message.

"Oh."

We sit in silence for a few minutes, neither one of us knowing what to say.

Ben finally gives me a funny look. "But, why do you have to sell your stuff?"

I lean back on the sidewalk with my hands behind my head. The smell of grass wafts on the wind. "I just want to help. That's all." My words sound empty. "If I can earn a little money, maybe it can make a difference."

"Hmmm." He studies me with what looks like pity. After a few long seconds, a smile grows on his lips. "Well, you have a hundred bucks."

He nudges my leg for encouragement. But it doesn't help.

"Yeah," I say staring up at the cottony clouds. "But, I should have gotten at least $150 for those two things."

The clouds transform into moving trucks as my mind wanders again to thoughts of New Jersey. I can't help it. The worry creeps back in any time I have a minute of silence.

Ben interrupts my nerve-wracking visions. "I'll buy your old Gameboy from you. How much do you want for it?" He has a smile in his voice and it tears my focus away from the clouds.

Tingles fly up and down my left arm as I stand and shake it to wake it up. "You can have the Gameboy for free," I tell him and walk back over to the tables.

Ben doesn't answer. I watch him a minute, hoping he'll say something. But he just stands on the sidewalk staring out into the street.

Without any customers and Ben's sudden silence, the empty quiet leaves me a bit nervous, so I pace behind the tables. Dragging my feet across the driveway, I enjoy the swishing sound my sneakers make against the concrete.

After 15 more minutes without customers, I finally grow tired of the noise. Surprised Ben hasn't said a word about it, I notice that he's moved to the grass, looking pretty comfortable with his eyes closed and his arms behind his head.

I clear my throat to get his attention.

No response.

I cough louder and he still doesn't move. Finally, I tap his arm with my foot. His eyes shoot open and he jumps to his feet.

His freaked-out reaction throws me into a howling laugh. He rubs his face and gives me a dirty look with a raised fist.

"You shouldn't have fallen asleep," I say between laughs.

"It was that noise you were making. It made me fall asleep," he says and plops back down into his spot. "Wake me up like that again and I'll tackle you."

"Yeah, right," I tell him and go back to the table.

When Ben grows quiet again and I can't figure out what else to do with myself, I notice that the action figures look lonely. I set up another battle scene and decide that it's time to

start a war.

I get at eye level with the toys and move them into position. First, GI Joe takes out a ninja. Then a cowboy ropes an Indian. When a squad of Army men are just about to attack the Navy Seals, a bunch of kids my age ride up on their skateboards and I drop the toys faster than if one of the Army men had shot me in the hand.

I recognize all the guys. Two of them are in seventh grade, just like me. Rudy and Max. Rudy is a tall, red-headed kid who looks like he works out. Max has a hard looking face, as if he's got a lot more on his mind than school and skateboarding.

47

Both are in my history class, but neither dude has ever talked to me. They're too cool.

They flip over their skateboards and stare out into the street, ignoring us.

I push out my chest, trying to look bigger, not like a little kid playing with action figures.

"Hey, Rudy." I wave and give a nod. "Hey, Max."

Both guys go straight for the Wii games, not acknowledging me at all.

"This your stuff?" Rudy finally asks after browsing through the games for a minute. He pushes his red hair out of his eyes. His thick arms catch my attention. Why has everyone hit their growth spurt except me?

"Uh, yeah, it's mine," I tell him. I hesitate to say more but I need the money. "You wanna buy something?"

Rudy doesn't answer. He flips through the games and then the CDs. I gulp down a knot growing in my throat.

Max is still quiet. He flicks one of my action figures and knocks it down. He smiles and then does the same thing to another one. Within a matter of seconds, he's knocked down all of them. With a satisfied look on his face, he walks to the curb and joins the other guys.

I glare at his back, feeling tension growing in my chest. I want to say something, to yell at him to come back and pick up my toys. I look at Ben and he's noticed, too. He stands next to me with his arms tight across his chest, looking tougher than me, the

HISTORY NERD.

He stares at Rudy who's been standing at the table for several minutes with a "Home Alone 3" DVD in his hand. Unlike Max, he's placed everything else back where he found it.

With Ben at my side and Max back on the sidewalk, I feel a bit bolder. "If you want that one, I'll sell it to you for five bucks."

He taps his finger on it and waits another few seconds. "Okay," he says and pulls a $5 bill out of his pocket. He hands it to me and looks me in the eye. "Thanks. My little brother will love this."

"Uh, sure," I say and stuff the bill in my pocket. I look at Ben and shrug, caught off guard by Rudy's friendliness.

Rudy walks back to his friends. Before he reaches the sidewalk, he turns around. "Hey, Jake. Uh, have you written your history report yet?"

The question, the fact that he even knows my name, takes me by surprise. I fumble my response. "Uh, um. Yeah. Uh … I'm almost done with it." I swallow to try to gain some self-control. "Why?"

He pauses and looks at the ground. "I was wondering if you could help me with mine." He looks up, shifts his gaze between me and his friends. "I mean, you always seem to get good scores on your history assignments."

I glance at Ben. His eyes grow big.

It's a strange turn of events. I hesitate, not knowing what to say. But somehow just the fact that he knows my name and is asking for my help has given me a lighter feeling in my chest. "Uh, I guess. Sure," I say.

Rudy smiles, his white teeth glowing. "Great! Thanks. Could we work on it tomorrow?"

I look at Ben again and he's shifting his gaze between Rudy and the other guys.

I scan my brain to see if I have any plans. Nothing comes to mind. Tomorrow's church but nothing else.

"Sure," I tell him and swallow again because my mouth has become drier than my mom's homemade bread. "Uh, maybe you can come over to my place?"

"Perfect," he says and walks back to the other guys.

As they walk away I hear my name come from the group and then a bunch of laughter follows.

Even Rudy is laughing and nudging one of the guys with his elbow as he looks back at me. Somehow, I don't feel as certain about getting together with him as I did **minutes ago.**

Chapter 7
Taking on Trouble

As Rudy and his friends ride away on their boards, I tap Ben to try to get his attention. Maybe he noticed their laughing. But he won't look at me and it sets me on edge.

"What's wrong?"

He fidgets with a ninja and watches the guys as they disappear down the street. "Nothin'," he says. "I just thought we were going to ride to the high school to shoot some hoops tomorrow after church."

I cringe. "Oh, yeah. I forgot."

Ben tosses the ninja back on the table. "Forget about it." He walks back to the sidewalk and sits down. "I don't get why you're going to help that guy anyway."

"It's just a history assignment," I say to his back.

Ben doesn't respond. His head moves back and forth as he watches more cars drive by while plucking at a blade of grass.

I sit down next to him. "What's the big deal?" I ask, still remembering the laughter I heard as the guys rode away.

While I'm waiting for Ben to say something, two

cars stop in front of his house. A family with twin boys about Alex's age pile out of one of the cars. They go straight for the action figures.

For the moment, I forget about Ben's silence and the guys' laughter. I hop up and go round the table again.

"You like those?" I ask the boys.

"I have some just like this," says one of them.

I look back and forth between the twins. I can't see how their parents tell them apart. They both have long brown hair that covers their left eye. They also have a big cowlick right at the top of their heads, making the hair stand up. The idea of having to plaster that thing down each day makes me chuckle.

At least they're wearing different colored shirts. The one in the red asks me, "How much for all of them?"

"I want some, too," says Blue Shirt Boy.

Their mom walks up behind them and eyes the toys with uncertainty.

"Can we get these, Mom?" asks Red Shirt.

"Hmm. I don't know. Let me think about it." She looks up at me. "How much?"

"They can have all of them for just …" I stop to calculate what I've already made. Only $105. "How about $7?"

Mom groans and walks away.

With my chance to make some cash at risk, I look up at the sky and smack my palms together, saying a quiet prayer. "Give me this sale, God!"

Not wanting them to leave, I grab the ninja and start a fight with the solider that Red Shirt has in his hand.

Red Shirt seems to like the idea and makes blasting noises at me. Blue Shirt gets in on it with his own Navy Seal and they team up against me.

BRRRRR, KABOOM!

"I'm hit!" I yell. My ninja grabs at his heart. "Egh … uh … aaaaahhh!"

The ninja falls to the ground, rolls onto his side and gags some more, "Uhhhh, aaahhhh!"

The twins giggle and throw their action figures on top of mine until he stops making noises.

"I give up. You two win."

The boys pat each other on the back, find their mom and beg her for the toys.

I wait at the table, lining up the figures again in perfect battle formation. I watch Mom shake her head, the boys pull at her arm, jump up and down and then give her a big hug. She reaches into her purse and pulls out a $5 and two $1 bills.

Third sale of the day!

Once the twins have taken off with their arms full of action figures, I still have a few more customers waiting. A lady about the same age as my mom has three Wii games in her hand and a $20 bill.

"Will you take $20 for all of these?" she asks.

I stick out my hand faster than a dog after bacon. "Sure."

I total everything in my head as she walks away. $132. Not too bad.

After another hour, I've sold just about everything except for my old Gameboy. Even the state quarters set earned me $5.

I pick up the Gameboy and sit down next to Ben on the sidewalk. He'd been sitting with his back to me since Rudy left.

"Here's the Gameboy." I hold it out to him.

"Huh?"

"Remember, I said you could have it."

"Oh. Yeah, whatever." He shrugs his shoulders.

"I even sold the quarters for $5." I laugh and give him a light punch on the arm while pulling my stash out of my pocket. "Can you believe it? $152!"

Ben looks at the money and then across the street.

I let out a loud breath, not sure how to get through to him. "Come on, man. What's wrong? I said I was sorry about tomorrow. I just forgot."

Ben sighs and gets up. "Yeah. Okay. No big deal." He walks back to the tables.

I watch him for a second, not sure whether he's still upset. He lays a table on its side and pushes the legs in. Then he organizes the few remaining toys, places them in a box and starts on another table. I get up and help him with it.

Once the second table is closed, Ben hits the clicker for his garage door. The odor of used cat litter wafts out and I hold my nose. At least it's a smell confined to the garage.

Inside the garage, we heft the tables around the family car and leave them next to a wall. Ben then sits on the car's bumper and stares back out to the street.

"You know, Rudy likes to hang out with those eighth graders," he says.

"Yeah." I sit down next to him and swing my legs back and forth, waiting.

"I heard that they're

trouble makers."

My legs swing even faster. "What kind of trouble?"

"Well, I just hear things." He pauses. "The other day someone told me that those guys grabbed little Bobby Richmond as he walked to school and took his lunch money."

"Really?" I jump down off the bumper and look at Ben. Bobby Richmond is only 10 years old. "Did Rudy do it too?"

"Uh. I don't know. That's just what I heard." He gets down. "I just don't think it's a good idea for you to hang out with him."

"We're not hanging out. I'm just going to help him with his project. That's all."

"Well, I just don't trust that guy. And you shouldn't either." Ben walks through the garage to the entry to the house.

Feeling like I have to defend myself, I grit my teeth and run my hands through my hair. "You're making a big deal out of nothing," I say to his back. It comes out sounding angry.

Ben turns and his face is tight. "Whatever." He shakes his head. "I gotta go. Catch ya later." He puts his hand on the garage door clicker and waits for me to move out of the way.

I frown but step out of the door's path. "Yeah. See ya."

Standing with my back to the street, I watch the door clunk shut. After staring at it a few seconds, I grab my bike off the lawn and head home. The uphill ride is slower than the ride there. It gives me plenty of time to think about just one thing …

should I trust Rudy?

Chapter 8
Games are Gone?

lex wakes me up banging on my door the next morning. "Time for church!" he yells.

I grunt and pull the covers over my head. I'm not ready to start another day. Saturday had been more work than I expected. After I got home from the yard sale, I'd crashed in my bed for a few hours. Then I woke up around dinner time, downed some soup and went right back to bed. Making money was more stressful than I expected.

I lie there a few minutes, hoping Alex will go away, but he keeps pounding. "Get out of here," I yell.

The next thing I know, he's knocking to the tune of "Mary Had a Little Lamb."

It's more than I can take.

I yell his name and try to throw the blankets off, but the sheet catches on my foot, so I roll off the bed and tumble to the floor. A garbled scream escapes my mouth.

AARGH!

I land in the middle of my coins again and immediately regret not cleaning them up.

Alex cracks open the door and peeks inside.

I groan at him. "What do you want?"

59

He takes that as an invitation to enter. "I got up before you!" He sports an ear-to-ear grin. "Bet you never thought that would happen." He dances around the room sticking his tongue out at me.

"What time is it?" I grunt.

"5:15!" He points at the digital clock on the dresser.

5:15?

My first thought is to throw the clock at him. I ball up my fists and take a deep breath before I say anything. "You woke me up to tell me that? I thought you said it was time for church?"

He stands over me. "You always get to choose the show because you're up first." He wags the remote control in my face and then points it at my TV. "Today, I'm in charge."

"You …" Before I can go on, sleepiness takes over and I interrupt myself with a big yawn. I stretch my arms over my head and then drop them to the floor, making a few coins bounce and jingle. "Whatever," I tell him.

Alex hops on my bed and fluffs a pillow. He must have surprised Wally because the dog jolts out from under the blankets and flies off the bed …

right onto my face.

"Ugh, Wally!" I push him off and hop onto the bed next to Alex.

He flips through the cartoon channels and stops at *Batman*. With a big smile, he sets the remote away from me and leans back with his hands behind his head.

I jab him in the ribs. "Don't get so comfortable."

Alex doesn't move. He giggles a little and keeps his eyes on the TV.

After a list of possible revenge ideas runs through my head, I decide to let it go. I lean back on the bed too, settling in.

We watch *Batman* in silence for a few minutes.

When the commercials start, Alex turns down the volume and looks at me. "Hey, have you seen my Wii basketball game?"

My breath catches and I wince. "Uh, why?" I picture the family who bought the video games and the money that's still inside my pant pocket.

"I wanted to play it yesterday. I couldn't find it. And the old bowling game is missing too."

I grab a pillow and toss it in the air. "I thought you never played those games anymore." I catch it on its way down and cover my face with it.

"I do, sometimes." Alex pulls the pillow off and looks at me with a scowl. "What did you do with them?"

I sit up and chuck the pillow into the hoop on the backside of my door. It lands on top and stays there.

"I sold them," I say in a quiet voice without looking directly at him.

"What?" Alex yells. "You sold my games? To who? For how much? Why?" The words fly out of his mouth faster than overcooked Brussels sprouts. He grabs my shoulders and turns me to look at him.

I try to shrug his hands away. "First of all, you have to promise not to tell Mom and Dad."

"Why?" He crosses his arms and stares at me.

Telling him what I've been up to would be a risk, so I pause to think.

Before I can make up my mind, he hurdles off the bed and toward the door.

"I'm telling!"

"Stop!" I grab his arm in desperation. "Okay, I'll tell you." Almost tripping over Wally, I lead him back to the bed.

I swallow hard and begin.

"I'm trying to earn money to help them until Dad finds a job." I let go of his arm when his eyes get big. "I just don't have much yet, so I'm not ready to tell them."

He's silent for a few long seconds. Finally, he chokes out an, "Oh." Then he looks at the floor for a minute. "How much did you sell them for?"

Pride wells up inside me and I rub my hands together in preparation to offer him the news. "Three games for $20."

"Three?" His eyes dart back and forth across my room. "What other game?"

"The carnival games." I let it out slow and wait for his reaction.

He shrugs. "I didn't like that game anyway."

My muscles feel light with relief. "You still going to tell?"

Alex shakes his head. "Don't worry about it." He lies down and grabs the remote again. "But, I get to choose the shows for the next month."

The smug look on his face says everything. He has the upper hand and he knows it. I can either accept his form of blackmail or let him tell my parents.

I have no choice.

I get back on the bed and watch *Batman* with a sinking feeling in my stomach for the next hour and a half.

When it's finally almost time for church, Alex leaves to get dressed. As he pulls my door closed, he pokes his head back in the room and gives me that smug look once again.

The thought of having to deal with that face for who-knows-how-long makes my whole body tense. I bite my tongue and don't say a word.

When he's gone, I pull on my dirty jeans and T-shirt from the day before. The money from the sale is still in my pocket so I pull it out and count it again.

still $152.

If I could earn that much in one day, I can't imagine how much I could come up with in a week. Or even two. Dealing with Alex could be worth it. I just need another plan.

"Jake! We're leaving," Mom yells down the hall, interrupting my thoughts.

I fold the money and stick it in my sock drawer. I scan my room for my Bible but don't see it.

"Jake!" Mom sounds impatient.

I move some dirty clothes but the Bible isn't there.

She yells again, "You better get out here right now!"

I push a few old homework assignments around

on the floor. "Ugh. Where is it?" I look under the bed and under my dresser.

Nothing.

Finally giving up, I run down the hall, hoping Mom isn't too upset about waiting.

She stands at the front door with her hands on her hips. "No Bible?"

I offer a nervous smile and shrug. Late for church, no Bible and Mom in a bad mood. Not a good way to start the day.

She shakes her head. "Let's go."

I fast-walk to the garage and hop in the back seat of the car. Dad gives me an irritated look but starts the car and we leave for church.

After a quiet ride, I jump out of the car and walk straight to youth group while my parents go to their morning Bible study. Hoping to talk to Ben about Rudy, I look for him on my way but don't see him.

When I open the door to the youth group building, Ben is the first person I notice. I raise my hand to wave, but he

turns his head away.

A ripple of nerves runs through me. When I sit next to him, Ben gives me a forced "hi" then turns his attention to the youth pastor who has just walked to the pulpit.

Forced to stay quiet during the sermon, I prickle with uncertainty the entire time. When the message ends, Ben goes to the front to ask a question. I wait for him outside hoping to talk to him. But he doesn't come out and I'm starting to wonder if he's purposefully avoiding me.

I stand at the door a few minutes and finally check my watch. With only two minutes until the main service starts, I can't wait any longer. If I'm late, Mom and Dad will kill me.

I peek inside the room and see Ben chatting with another kid who he's never talked to before. I try to catch his eye but he won't look my direction. Not wanting to leave without talking to him, I lean into the room. "Hey, Ben!"

He turns and gives me a weak smile. "Uh, catch

you later. I need to talk to Greg for a minute."

Greg? I didn't think he knew the kid's name.

"Oh, okay." I let the door close and stand staring at it another minute. When it swings open and almost hits me in the nose, I snap out of my zombie-like state and go to the main sanctuary. By the time I get there, nervous energy runs through my right leg and I can't get it to stop twitching.

It's all Ben's fault.

If he'd just act normal, everything would be okay.

Although, maybe I could've had a better attitude when he warned me about Rudy. I just don't know what to think about that guy.

I enter the large sanctuary and sit in the pew near my parents but as far away from Alex as I can. When the worship music ends, I try to focus on the message but I can't. Mom reaches out a few times to calm my leg but it doesn't help. I doodle on the church bulletin, take deep breaths and try to forget about Ben for the moment.

Just as I'm about to draw a moustache on Pastor Simon's picture, I hear the word "coin" from the pulpit.

I look up to the screen to check and it says the verses can be found in the book of Luke. I reach for my Bible to learn more about this coin. Too bad I left it at home.

Mom must have seen me reach because she shakes her head and frowns. I sigh, giving myself a mental reminder to find the Bible when I get home. Maybe I could check out the coin verses later.

In the meantime, I tune back in to Pastor Simon's story about a woman who sounds a lot like me. She lost a coin and cleaned every bit of her house looking for it. The party she threw when she found it sounded like a blow-out.

The last time I lost one of my coins I made my room spotless trying to find it. And just like the woman, I had a party. It was just Wally and me, but it was a party. I smile at the thought of dancing around my room with the dog.

I'm still daydreaming about my Wally party when we get home, so I grab him and a few of his favorite treats and go to my room. We play fetch for almost an hour.

As I'm about to teach Wally a new trick, Mom taps on my door and leans her head in. "There's a kid named Rudy at the door who says that you're supposed to help him with some homework today."

I freeze.

I'd forgotten all about Rudy. And now I don't know if I even want to

Chapter 9
Tutoring Time

"I can't believe he's here," I whisper to myself and feed Wally another treat.

Mom crinkles her nose like she smells something bad and looks around my room. "So, are you going to help him?"

The temptation to leave him there hits me. Maybe I could forget all about the tutoring and act like I never offered.

But, I promised I'd help. And he didn't seem like the kind of guy that Ben said he was. He'd been pretty nice at the yard sale and even bought games for his little brother. A guy who's willing to do that couldn't be that bad.

"So?" Mom interrupts my thoughts and rubs her nose trying to hide the disgusted look on her face.

Wally nips at my fingers asking for more treats. I give him one more and pat his head as I look around my room and take a whiff, too. I blow the air back out as quick as I can. The room smells like dog treats and sweat. "Can we work at the kitchen table?"

Mom pinches her nose. "I hope so," she says and walks out.

I close up my room and follow her. The front door is wide open and Rudy stands there with a big red binder in his hand that matches his hair.

I bite my lip at the sight of him. We never really

talked to each other before the yard sale. I shift on my feet feeling a bit awkward. "Um, come on in?" It comes out sounding more like a question than an invitation.

He takes a step forward, over the threshold. "Thanks for helping me," he says with a smile. "I'm no good at history. I get all the dates and people mixed up."

His smile sets me more at ease. "No problem." I gesture for him to follow me to the kitchen. The room still smells like the leftover spaghetti from lunch. A much better odor than in my room.

Mom smiles at Rudy. "You can sit here." She picks up some bills off the table and wipes it down for us.

I can't help thinking about the last thing Ben said about Rudy. I eye him as he waits for Mom to finish up. He doesn't look like a

trouble-maker.

"You boys want something to drink?" Mom asks as she stacks the bills and puts them on the counter.

"Sure," I say.

"No, thank you." Rudy is even polite.

Mom takes a Coke out of the fridge and hands it to me. She gives another one to Rudy. "Just in case you get thirsty."

"Thank you, Mrs. King," he says and sits down. Not even Ben had ever been so polite to my mom.

She smiles and pats him on the back. "Aren't you a nice boy?"

At that comment, my cheeks grow hot and I look at Rudy to see his reaction. Mom has gone too far, treating him like a little kid.

Rudy doesn't react. He just smiles and places his binder on the table.

His response lessons my embarrassment. It's not every day I have someone new at the house and I don't want Mom to ruin it.

I grab a pencil and fidget a bit. "So, what are you doing your report on?"

"Mr. Birgdon gave us so many topics to choose from, I don't know which one I should do." He opens his binder and pulls out the assignment sheet.

Remembering that the assignment is due on Friday, I cringe. "You mean you haven't even

started yet?

Rudy looks away. "No."

"You know it's due this week, right?" I tap my pencil on the table, starting to feel that nervous energy coming back.

"Yeah, I know." His voice is calm. He doesn't seem worried at all. "That's why I asked for help." He looks at Mr. Birgdon's list. All the ancient civilizations are there: Egypt, Greece, China, and Rome. I already finished my report on ancient Rome. Of course, I chose it because of their cool coins.

"What do you think of that idea?" Rudy asks me.

"Huh? What idea?" I guess he must have said something while I was daydreaming about the Roman coins. I hadn't heard a word.

"I said that I thought of doing it on Egypt."

"Uh, yeah. Ancient Egypt is cool."

He flips through the assignment papers and lets out a breath. "I just don't know where to start."

My leg starts jittering along with my pencil tapping. Rudy has so many hours of research and writing to do. And he only has five days to finish it. If I were him, I'd be a mess.

I stare at him a moment, trying to judge what's going on inside his mind. Trying to figure out if he cares at all that he only has five days to do such a big assignment. There isn't an ounce of fear in his eyes. His hands are solid and his legs don't show a bit of jitters.

He's nothing like me, I decide.

"If I were you, I'd just Google ancient Egypt to start," I tell him.

He looks around the kitchen. "Do you guys have a computer?"

"Oh, yeah." I go looking for Mom and find her folding laundry in her room. "Hey, Mom. Can we use your laptop?"

She lays one of Dad's shirts across the bed. "Sure, I left it sitting on your dad's big chair in the living room." As she flattens a towel and folds it in half, she reminds me again "what a nice boy" Rudy is. I nod and walk back to the living room.

I find the laptop sitting right where Mom said, in direct view of my seat next to Rudy. I hadn't even noticed.

"This is going to take a while, isn't it?" Rudy asks as he flips through his papers again.

I lift my shoulders as if to say, "I don't know." But I can't lie to him. "Yeah. You're going to have to work on it every day after school until Friday," I tell him.

He sets the papers down and reaches into his back pocket. "Could you help me? I mean, could you help me every day this week? I'll even pay you." He pulls out a wallet. "My Mom gave me enough to pay you

I blink hard and force myself to swallow.

He holds up two $20 bills. I think of the money I already have in my sock drawer. If I add his forty dollars, it would bring me up to $192.

Just when I'm about to say yes, something stops me. It's a thought, a vague reminder of something Pastor Simon said a long time ago. It had something to do with not expecting anything in return when you do a favor for someone else.

I wrack my brain trying to figure out where that thought came from. I don't even remember when Pastor Simon said it.

Rudy waves the money in front of me again. "Please?"

I think about Pastor Simon again but I

reach out for the money anyway.

Chapter 10
Give Back the Bucks

After I stuff Rudy's forty bucks in my pocket, I stick a bag of popcorn in the microwave, set it to cook and turn my attention to Rudy. I plug in Mom's laptop and open it.

"Just do a Google search for ancient Egypt," I tell him.

Rudy shakes his head. "Sheesh! Sounds a lot easier than it did when Mr. Birgdon gave us the assignment."

He clicks a few buttons to get to the Internet and then types in his search information. Right when the results list appears, the computer screen goes black.

We look at each other and then at the computer. The plug looks okay, so I hit a few buttons and nothing happens.

Rudy looks at me and I see uncertainty in his eyes, maybe even a bit of fear. "What are we going to do now?" He taps a few more buttons. "How am I going to get my report done without a computer?"

We sit in silence staring at the screen until a foul odor walks up my nostrils and punches them in the face.

The popcorn!

I jump up and run to the microwave to stop the cooking. When I pull it open, smoke pours out along with an even heavier dose of the crispy smell.

"Yuck! I hate the smell of burnt popcorn," Rudy says. He moves out of the kitchen and stands in the hallway watching me, arms across his chest.

With Rudy staring me down, the tightness growing in my chest feels as if Darth Vader has my heart in a choke hold.

I fumble with the popcorn bag, trying not to burn myself, and yank open the kitchen window. Pulling open the back door, I set the bag on the porch, and pray the smell will leave with it.

Once the bag is out of the room, Rudy comes back and takes a seat in front of the computer. His lips are tight and he's pinching his nose.

I take a deep breath, put another bag of popcorn in the microwave and sit back down next to him.

"Let's try again," Rudy says, sounding like a chipmunk.

I nod and he slowly releases the grip on his nose. We both take turns unplugging the computer and plugging it back in. Then we try our hands at turning it off and on, taking out the battery pack and trying again.

Nothing works.

Before trying one last time, I take a peek toward the microwave. When the popping of the corn slows a bit, I jump up and pull it out before I repeat the burning incident. I pour the perfect buttery kernels into a bowl.

Even though the kitchen smells like ashes and the computer is broken, at least we have something to eat.

I set the bowl between us but Rudy doesn't even look at it. There's a growing look of frustration in his eyes as he taps the screen, telling it,

"Come on, come On, come on."

After cramming a handful of popcorn into my mouth, I wipe the butter on my pants and close the laptop. "Just hold on," I tell him.

I walk back toward Mom's room hoping she'll have some answers. It isn't until I'm halfway there that I remember the $40 in my pocket. The once crisp bills have now been wadded in my pants for at least 15 minutes. I stop and pull them out.

Both bills are crinkled like an old set of notes. But money is money. I stare down at them and then lift them to my nose and smell. That dirt, sweat, and ink aroma never gets old.

I take one more long whiff and the popcorn and ashes odor mixes with the money. The thought of Rudy sitting at the table, his eyes big in fear over his report, brings a lump to my throat. He needs help and all I can think about are the two $20s in my hand.

Disgusted with myself, I stuff the money back into my pocket and go to the kitchen. Rudy is at the table with his head in his hands.

I clear my throat to get his attention. When he lifts his head, the look on his face convinces me.

"Here's your money back." I whip it out and push

it toward him. "I can't take it."

When he doesn't reach for it, I set the bills on the table in front of him.

Rudy's mouth falls open. His eyes shift to me and then to the money. "What am I supposed to do now?" He huffs then forces his chair back from the table, slams his binder shut and grabs the money.

His reaction makes me lurch and I think of Ben's warning. I'm still not sure what kind of guy Rudy is, but at the moment, the scowl on his face tells me he's one unhappy guy.

He moves toward the door.

I scratch my head in confusion. I thought he would be happy to get the money back. I try to stop him. "What's wrong?"

Rudy turns and his eyes flash with anger. When he looks at me I feel like I need to hide. "I guess I'll have to find someone else to help me," he says and keeps walking.

I let out a gasp then jump between him and the door. "Stop!"

He gives me that look again and it makes me squirm on the inside.

"I mean ... that's not what I mean."

I take a deep breath and try to avoid his death stare. "I want to help you. No money. Just as a friend."

The death stare disappears. "Really?" A small smile creeps into his eyes.

"Uh, yeah." I move away from the door and motion for him to follow me back to the kitchen. "Come on." I turn my head to see if he's coming. For a few seconds he stands at the door but then walks back to the kitchen.

We sit down at the table again and I open the laptop.

"Remember, it's broken," Rudy says and grabs a handful of popcorn.

I had completely forgotten about our computer problem. I look at him. He's munching slow and relaxed now.

I hit the ENTER button, not knowing what else to do, and the screen lights up. We both look at each other in shock. I give a light tap to the Internet button, trying not to do anything to break it again. It works so I try the Google search and it comes back with thousands of results for ancient Egypt.

"Yes!" Rudy pounds his fist on the table. The force sends the popcorn bowl over the side. He cringes and looks at me. "Oops."

I burst out in a laugh and Rudy chuckles, too. We both spend the next few minutes crawling around picking up the popcorn, laughing at the confusion of the last few minutes.

Once the popcorn is back in the bowl, we spend the next three hours with our heads at the computer. Rudy scrolls through websites and I help him figure out what's important and what's not. He listens to everything I say, never questioning my advice, and takes notes like I'm the

president of the United States.

By the time Mom announces dinner, my chest is so puffed out with pride that I probably look like I think I really am the president of the United States.

Mom leans over our work. "Hmmm," she says as she eyes Rudy's notes. "Looks like you're doing a good job. Would you like to stay and eat with us?"

Rudy's face grows red and he looks at his watch.

"I didn't realize what time it was. Sorry, I've gotta go."

He scans the table full of books and papers that we've been working with. "Uh, do you think we could do this tomorrow night and Tuesday night too?" Then he looks at Mom, "I promise I won't interrupt dinner again."

Mom laughs and wipes her hands on a towel. "You don't bother us at all. You can come over any time." She takes a large spoon and stirs the pot of mashed potatoes on the stove. Then she leans over to me and whispers in my ear.

"So polite."

Rudy looks to me. I can feel the smile growing on my face. "Sure, come over after school for the next couple days and we'll get it done."

It's as if I promised to buy Rudy a new skateboard. He high-fives me and smiles from ear to ear. He stuffs a few of the papers into his red notebook and walks toward the door. "Great! I'll see you tomorrow."

After I say goodbye to Rudy and close the door, I do a little dance. I go to the kitchen and clean the rest of the homework papers and computer off the table. I stack them in a pile on the counter and then help Mom set out the dishes so we can eat.

"You're in a good mood," she tells me. "Not even one complaint about setting the table."

Usually, I'd rather do anything than set the table. Tonight, I couldn't care less about the chore.

When I sit down to dinner and I'm still smiling, Dad notices. "What's up with you," he asks over the meatloaf.

I just shrug. I nod toward the stack of homework and the computer.

"That was fun."

Alex laughs and milk comes out of his nose. "You're the only one who would think that doing history for three hours is fun."

Mom and Dad look at each other and Dad tosses a napkin Alex's way.

I scrunch my eyebrows at Alex. "Maybe it's fun to help someone," I tell him, my voice sounding angrier than I'd meant.

Alex keeps his

mouth shut after that.

Chapter 11
Report's Ready

y the time Wednesday rolls around, Rudy's report on Egypt is probably better than what I wrote for Rome.

When he sends it to Mom's printer, I stand there waiting for it, biting my nails. The printer sputters and spits it out and I pull it off the minute it's done.

The report is clear, interesting, and basically perfect. I feel a twinge of jealousy at first but when Rudy sidles up next to me and starts reading, too, I see that big smile grow on his face again. Those jealous feelings

do a disappearing act.

"Here you go." I hand him the four pages and give him a pat on the back. "You did a great job!"

Rudy handles the pages like they belong in a museum and places them in his notebook. "Yeah. This is the best report I've ever done."

I BET IT IS, I think.

As soon as those words run through my head, I clench my jaw and remind my brain to shut its mouth.

"Thanks again," Rudy says and goes to the door.

"You're welcome," I tell him. He walks with a spring in his step and there's no way I can keep those jealous feelings going. The more I watch him and his smile that never leaves, the lighter I feel.

"You did a great job," I tell him and I mean it.

He turns and holds his hand up for a high-five. "You're pretty cool, man," he says.

There's a knot in my throat all of a sudden. I can barely lift my arm to smack his hand because I'm so stricken with shock. No one has ever told me I'm cool before. No one besides Ben, that is.

After I stand staring at him for a few seconds, he lets his hand fall. I miss my chance to follow-through on one of the best high-fives ever.

"Catch you around," he says and then he's out the door. He doesn't turn back and ask for another high-five. He just walks away with his red binder under his arm.

I'm left standing, staring at his back, wishing I hadn't been such a nerd when someone finally called me COOL.

With my hand still on the door, I remember Ben, which sends another knot into my throat. I can hardly swallow the more I think of him.

It's been four days since the yard sale. I tried to call him the last two nights, but he didn't answer his phone.

At school he has yet to say a word to me. Despite having several classes together, he managed to avoid me and escape class before I had a chance to catch him.

As I grow more upset thinking about Ben,

my grip tightens on the door handle.

I watch Rudy's back as he slips into the distance and then I peel my hand loose, sliding the door closed.

I sit on the edge of Dad's recliner and punch in Ben's phone number again. When he doesn't answer for the third time this week, I slam the phone down.

All those positive feelings–everything I'd spent the last hours building–and the good stuff I had inside is now

Smashed, flat and gone.

I retreat to my bedroom and crawl under the covers in bed, feeling the muscles in my face tightening. After half an hour I'm still awake with thoughts of Ben and Rudy. The only way I can get myself to stop worrying is to make a plan to force Ben to talk to me.

Tomorrow I'd put the plan into action. If I had to follow him home to get his attention, I would.

The next morning I wake up late and race to get dressed. I arrive at school just in time to see Ben enter homeroom as the first bell rings. I enter the room, considering how to get Ben's attention. Once the bell sounds, Mr. Bowen won't allow even a whisper.

Despite being desperately aware of Mr. Bowen's "no-talking" policy, I try to get Ben to respond by staring him down. When it doesn't work, I decide to try again at lunch while sitting a few tables away. That doesn't work either. His face is like stone and he never once looks my way.

He's surrounded by a group of guys from the baseball team who have never talked to me. For some reason, Ben seems to have all day to talk to them. Irritated, I stuff the last half of my sandwich in my mouth and decide I'd have to wait until school is over to go through with my plan.

When Ben leaves school after the final bell, I throw my hoodie over my head, put my head down and follow him, keeping about twenty feet back. After the first five minutes, I get distracted when I catch sight of a penny in the gutter. I sidetrack for a second, grab it and stuff it in my pocket. Only seconds later, I almost step on another.

Within the next ten minutes, I find seven more pennies and almost forget my plan to get Ben to talk. When I finally look up, I catch him peeking back at me a few times. He knows I'm there, but he's still

ignoring me.

Ben's cold shoulder doesn't stop me though. I keep my distance and when he goes inside his house, I wait. Within seconds, I see the whites of his eyes peeping out from the sheer curtains in his living room.

Still standing on the sidewalk, I wave and smile at him. He shuts the curtains with a snap and the front door opens. "What?" He pokes his head out with his dark hair falling over his glasses.

"What's going on?" I cuff my hands around my mouth. "Why won't you talk to me?"

"Just forget about it, Jake," he says. "Go home."

"Nope." I fold my arms and sit on the grass. "I'm staying right here until you tell me what's up."

"Ugh." Ben slams the door so hard it rattles.

Not discouraged, I sit. When time drags on, I finally think about going home. Just as I'm about to

walk away, I hear the door open again.

Ben yells from behind the screen, "Get in here!"

I sprint to the door and he lets me in. He sits in his usual spot on the flowered sofa near the window and I take the spot he always reserves for me on a brown fluffy chair.

Ben crosses his arms and glares at me. I bristle with those mad eyes staring me down. But I take a deep breath and get a whiff of the cookie-scented candles his Mom uses. (Definitely better than the cat smell in their garage.)

"So? What's the problem?" I ask once my heartbeat slows a bit.

"The problem is ...

your new friend Rudy."

He spits out the name *Rudy* as if it tastes like dirt in his mouth.

The sound of it makes me shudder. "I thought you said it wasn't a big deal if I helped him."

"At first it wasn't." He stares out the window and a big frown grows on his face. "Until Monday."

I gulp. "What happened Monday?"

Ben takes a breath. "Well ... I was on my way to math class and Rudy and his friends were hanging around by the bathroom."

He stands and moves to the middle of the room. "So I was about to go in, but decided not to and turned around, like this." He acts out the scene. "That guy Max was right next to me. As I started walking away he stuck out his leg, like this." He stretches out his leg.

"And?"

"I didn't see it." He shakes his head. "I know, I know I should have. But I didn't and I tripped." He mocks falling onto the ground face first.

"Ooh." I sink back into the chair, putting my hand over my eyes and peeking through my fingers.

"But that's not the worst of it." He lays flat on the

tile floor with his arms and legs spread out like a starfish. "I was on the ground like this. My books went everywhere. And Rudy and his friends stood there and laughed."

I close my fingers in front of my eyes and groan. "I'm sorry. Why didn't you tell me? What did you do?"

When I pull my hands down, he's up from the floor, dusting himself off. "I didn't do anything. It's not worth it to fight them."

"You're big enough. You could have," I say.

"Well, I didn't want to start anything with your new friend," he uses his fingers like he's putting quotes around the word "friend."

"I was just helping him with his homework." I swallow hard. "And besides, he's been nice to me."

Ben sits down next to me and gives me a funny look. "I wouldn't be so sure about Rudy." He looks me in the eyes. "While they were having such a great time laughing at me, I heard one of those guys say your name. And Rudy just

kept on laughing."

Chapter 12
Freaky Friend

After my talk with Ben, things still feel tense between us. When I leave his house he gives me a weak smile and says, "Talk to you soon." Whatever that means.

I spend half the night awake again. There had to be an explanation for Rudy laughing with the other guys. Some kind of excuse for the way they treated Ben.

I toss and turn but eventually fall asleep late into the night. When I wake up the next morning, I feel as heavy as a bag full of dirty laundry.

Trying to stay awake for the rest of the school day would be a challenge. After a slow morning, dragging myself to get ready, I leave Alex at the elementary school and walk toward the junior high.

It's a typical San Francisco foggy day. The mist is low to the ground, keeping the air cool. It's the kind of day that makes me want to curl up on the couch in front of the TV. Not the best weather when I have to sit through seven periods of class on three hours of sleep.

Throughout the day, I move from class to class in a haze. Most of what I hear from my teachers sounds the same. They all—Mr. Birgdon, Mrs. Ransom, Mr. Bowen—sound like a buzzing bunch of bumblebees.

By the time the last bell finally sounds, I can't wait to get home and lay my head on my pillow. Feeling grateful that it's Friday, I start toward home and kids move past me in a hurry. Despite walking like a turtle, I keep moving until I see something that wakes me up faster than a pile of

Halloween candy.

It's Rudy, Max and their friends and they're walking a short distance ahead of me.

My brain kicks into working mode. My heart pounds in a heavy rhythm like I've been given a shot of Coca-Cola right in the arm. I'm alert to everything around me.

I notice the flies flitting past my head and the sun beating down on my sweatshirt. The conversations of other kids as they pass me become a part of my thoughts; but I try to zone in on what's going on with Rudy and his friends.

Max runs ahead of the other guys and then slides on a bunch of dirt, like he's sliding into home base. One of the other guys mimics him but ends up going too fast, falls and lands on his backside.

The guys laugh at him and I watch to see how he reacts. He rubs himself for a second and then bursts out laughing too. Max holds a hand out to him and helps him off the ground.

I study them for a while, keeping my distance. They look like they're having a blast. Every few minutes they slap each other on the back and give high-fives like the one I missed the other day.

Part of me wants to catch up with them. I could join them, become one of their group. Just hang out like another one of the "cool" guys.

Another part of me can't stop thinking about Max tripping Ben and then everyone laughing. Maybe even laughing about me.

After taking it all in, I pick up my pace and catch up with the group. In a casual sort of way, I try to join them.

"What's up?" I give them all a chin nod as I fall in step with them.

Max and Jimmy are the first to glance my way. Max glares at me, studying me from head to toe. Then he turns away and ignores me. Jimmy does the same.

Rudy starts to say, "What's up?" but Max interrupts him and whispers something in his ear. Rudy watches me as he listens.

Everyone has stopped walking at this point. They're now in a circle and I'm on the outside of it. I stand there tapping my toe as

my nervous leg ramps up.

Jimmy and the other two guys start a conversation of their own while Max and Rudy continue their whispering. Max glances my way every couple seconds but I can't read the look on his face. He almost looks like he just swallowed rotten milk.

Waiting for several minutes for someone to acknowledge my existence leaves me sweaty and shaking all over. With twitching arms, I try to pull off my hoodie but it gets stuck on my head.

Feeling like a character in a bad comedy, I finally yank the sweatshirt off. The guys finish their whispering and Max makes a rude chuckle.

Rudy turns and looks at me, still standing outside their circle. But he doesn't make eye contact. Instead, his eyes dart from here to there.

"Uh, we gotta go," he says. "Catch ya later." Then all five of them kick into gear and leave me in the dust.

I watch the back of their heads as they move away in the opposite direction. They're fast, seeming to want to get away from me as quick as they can. My chest deflates and I feel like I did on my last birthday when I opened my biggest present and found just a bunch of socks.

It's not the reaction I expected and my tiredness sets in again. The longer I stand there, watching them turn into the size of ants as they slide into the distance, the heavier I feel. When I can no longer see them, my legs tell me that it's time to go home.

The closer I get to my house, the more that deflated feeling is replaced by a growing feeling of wanting to punch someone.

Little by little and with each heavy step, I recite another reason for my growing anger.

Stomp. They laughed at Ben.

Stomp. Maybe they laughed at me.

Stomp. Rudy didn't act like a friend.

Stomp. Max.

Max. I don't need a reason to be mad at him. All I need is to think about his face and I'm ready to rumble.

By the time I open my front door, my fists are in balls and every muscle in my body feels tense. I throw my backpack on the floor and fall into Dad's chair.

I flip on the TV and scroll through the channels, trying to forget about THOSE guys.

I've only been surfing through possible shows for a few minutes when Dad comes in from the backyard.

"I didn't know you were home," he says.

I keep my eyes on the screen. "Yeah. Just got

here."

"So, are you ready?" He stands between me and the TV with his arms folded.

I try to see around him, not really in the mood to talk. "Ready for what?"

When he makes a grunting sound and moves a little closer, completely blocking my view, I finally make eye contact.

"You're spending the weekend at your grandpa's in Sacramento. Didn't you remember?"

I throw my head back and look at the ceiling. It's the day of our monthly trip to Grandpa Lou's. With all the worry about Ben, Rudy, Max and Dad's lack of a job,

"Sure, I remembered," I lie. "I just thought I'd catch a little TV time before I get everything ready to go."

I try to peer around Dad again but he yanks the remote out of my hand and clicks off the TV.

"Jake, if you ever want to watch TV again you better get in your room and pack your things." He checks his watch. "Grandpa will be here in an hour and your brother is already set to go."

I take a heavy breath and jump out of Dad's chair. With my mind whirling, I stomp down the hall to my room to gather my things.

How is it that Alex gets help packing his clothes

but I have to do it myself? So what if he's 9 years old! If he can beat my score at just about every video game we have, I'm sure he can stuff some socks and underwear into a backpack.

I huff as I rip through the junk on my closet floor, looking for an extra pair of pants. I find them and toss them onto the desk by my bed. They land on top of my phone and it crashes to the floor.

I pick up the phone to set it back on the desk. Looking at it makes me want to call Rudy, just to see what he'd do. Just to see if he'd talk to me or if he'd give me the same reaction I got on the way home.

I start to make the call but then stop midway, uncertain what to do. Rudy had just become a puzzle that I couldn't figure out. He seemed like a great guy every time he came over. It had only been two days since he'd been sitting at my kitchen table telling me what a cool guy I am.

Had things changed that fast?

Calling Rudy could answer my questions or it could make things worse. And I decide that I'm not ready for

worse.

I push my pants aside and set the phone down. Instead of trying to figure Rudy out, I grab my overnight pack off my closet shelf and cram some clothes inside. Then I throw the pillows from my bed onto the floor and jump up and down on them pretending they're Rudy's face.

After ten minutes of this imaginary pummeling, I'm breathing so heavy that I have to stop.

I plop down in the middle of the pillows and try to catch my breath. Trying to deal with Rudy by pretending to smash his face hasn't helped me to feel any better. I'm still confused and he still acted like a freak!

And I still have that building urge to talk to him.

I stare at the phone again for a minute and finally pick it up. Puzzle or no puzzle, I just have to call.

I tap in Rudy's number from memory and wait. He picks up on the fifth ring, right when

I'm about to hang up.

"Hello?" It's Rudy's voice. It sounds normal. Like the nice guy he seemed to be.

"Uh, it's me Jake." I'm still sitting on the mound of pillows that I imagined to be his face.

"Uh, yeah. Could I call you later?" he says.

In the background, I hear other kids' voices. Someone asks him who he's talking to.

"I gotta go," Rudy says and then he hangs up.

I hold the phone out from my ear and stare at it. The empty dial tone answers me back.

"Call me later? Really?" I tell the phone. Then I smack it back on the desk and punch a pillow.

I pace back and forth for a few minutes, kicking my books out of my way. The thumping of my heart slows a little but my hands won't stop shaking.

"Whatever!" I yell at the phone and search for something to do with myself to keep my mind off of Rudy.

I grab my special Mason jar full of coins and dump them onto my bed. I fidget with them until my hands slow—no longer looking like the cause of a mini earthquake.

I find a few that I want Grandpa to take a look at, seeing that he knows more about coins than anyone on the planet. Just as I stuff them in my pocket, I hear Grandpa pull up outside and honk. I put the rest of the coins back in the jar, grab my pack and run outside.

I massage the coins in the palm of my hand as we drive to Sacramento. With the possibility that Grandpa might fill me in on the designs of these old nickels and pennies, I might just be able to keep my mind off Rudy and my constant wondering if he's

Chapter 13
Good ol' Grandpa

When I pull open the door to Grandpa's backyard, the aroma of apples floats on the breeze. The biggest limb from the neighbor's apple tree hangs down into Grandpa's yard filled with ripe fruit.

A crowd of chirping birds calls to me and I take a look around the yard with a smile. Downtown Sacramento is so different from San Fran. More spaces between the houses. No traffic noise. No exhaust fumes. Just a nice spot to relax and forget about Rudy, and the tension with Ben.

I pull an old lounge chair onto the lawn and lay with my feet up and my hands hooked behind my head. Within minutes, Alex ruins the quiet when he barrels out the back door with his harmonica blaring.

I give him a mad look, hoping he'll go away, but he roams the entire yard, flailing his arm in the air like he's in a parade. After a few minutes, I fling my legs over the side of the chair. "Stop, Alex!"

He quits blowing. "I'm just celebrating," he says. Then he smiles at me like he knows something I don't.

"Grrrrr," I grunt and look for something to throw at him. "What?"

"We're going to Old Town!" He flies at me and grabs my arm, jerking it up and down. "Let's go," he says. "We're leaving right now."

I pry my arm from his clutches. "Okay, okay. I'm

coming." I take a final look around my peaceful yard turned music hall. "I'll be back," I tell the tree and the birds.

I stride toward the house and Alex skips alongside me. "Grandpa said he'll buy us ice cream," he says.

If I had to leave my paradise for a while,

ice cream would make it worth it.

Grandpa waits for us in his gold Saturn station wagon, whistling a tune. "If you want ice cream, let's get going," he says as we mosey out of the house.

It takes less than ten minutes to reach our destination. Grandpa turns onto one of the old, cobblestone streets and slows the car behind a horse-drawn carriage. The sound of the horse's hooves makes me feel like I'm back in the gold rush days when this part of Sacramento was filled with prospectors.

When Grandpa pulls into a parking spot, I hop out onto the wooden sidewalk. I'm immediately reminded of the only thing I don't like about Old Town. The slatted walkway looks cool but it makes it hard to find coins. "Last time I didn't find more than a few pennies here," I tell Grandpa.

"Good luck today," he says and pats me on the back.

I follow him in the direction of the ice cream shop, keeping my eyes on the ground.

"There's no way you'll find anything today," Alex says and pokes me in the ribs.

I look at him and that silly grin makes me want to prove him wrong. "I bet I can find at least fifty cents today," I say to him and poke him back. Besides, any amount of money could be added to my stash for Mom and Dad.

I shouldn't have thought of Mom and Dad's money problems because it

makeS me Shudder.

The $152 I have in my sock drawer isn't enough to help them. Part of me wonders whether I should have taken the money Rudy offered.

I stop in my tracks. I shouldn't be thinking about Rudy right now either. It's all Alex's fault. If it hadn't been for him, I wouldn't be thinking about Mom and Dad, Rudy or anything else.

I pull my cell phone out to see if Rudy's called and the log is empty. I picture him having a good time with Max and the urge to jump on a pillow hits me again.

Just as I'm starting to entertain more ugly thoughts about Rudy, Alex sticks out his hand. "That's a bet," he says. "If I win, you do the dishes tonight."

Could it be possible to find fifty cents during the next few hours? I shake his hand, not wanting to give him the satisfaction of being right. "And if I win, you have to clean up."

We squeeze each other's hand and I force his arm

up and down, glad to have something to distract me from thoughts of Rudy.

Grandpa shakes his head at us and keeps walking. We follow him but I keep my eyes on the sidewalk. The worn planks of wood sit nestled together with small one inch openings between them. It's the perfect amount of space for a coin to roll away underneath.

I'm biting my lip halfway to the ice-cream store, wishing I hadn't made the bet. People shuffle past me and I try to avoid them without looking up. But before I can move out of her way, I run smack into a girl my age.

I look up into her eyes. They're a greenish-hazel color that reminds me of the apple tree in Grandpa's yard. Her hair is cut short into a mini-afro and her skin is the color of dark caramel.

For a second, I can't move. I can't stop looking at her until I realize that she's staring at me

like I'm an alien.

"Jake!" I hear Alex's voice through my haze.

I try to step around the girl, but she steps the same way as me. Then I try to move the other way and she does the same and we both almost run into a large planter.

Suddenly, we're in a stand-off, next to the planter, not moving. She starts giggling and I freeze.

"What are you doing?" I hear Alex again.

The girl and I look over to him at the same time. Alex's eyes grow big. He looks at the girl, back at me and then back at the girl.

She giggles again and then steps around me and disappears. I'm still frozen when Alex steps in front of me in her place. "She was pretty, huh?"

I shake my head to clear my thoughts.

"She was, wasn't she?" Alex taunts me.

I can't help looking behind me to see where she went. I turn just in time to see her step into a store across the street.

When Alex moves closer and smiles in my face, I push him away. I don't have time to think about girls. I have enough problems right now.

I look down and plan to keep moving, but right away I see the glint of a penny. I can only see half of it, but it's definitely a penny. The other half is stuck under the planter.

If I hadn't almost run into the girl, I never would have seen it. I glance back her way again and offer a silent

THANK YOU.

I bend down and try to nudge the penny out with a finger but it won't budge. Lacking leverage, I use both index fingers and push the penny with all my strength.

Before I know it, I'm lying flat and the penny is flying through the air. As my head hits the ground, I hear it "clink" against the glass door of a shop.

"Jake!" I look up and see Grandpa standing over

me. His eyes are as big as silver dollars. I smile up at him. "Oops."

He holds out a hand for me. "What now?"

I grab his hand and let him lift me up. Once I'm on my feet I run to the shop door. The penny lays right in the entryway, waiting for me.

I snatch it, make sure I don't have any holes in my pocket and pop it in. I give Grandpa and Alex a big smile. "Only 49 cents to go."

My smile disappears when I see the girl with the

apple-tree eyes

watching me from across the street. She holds her hand to her mouth and giggles even more.

"I'll show you," I whisper to Alex. "Before we go home, my pocket will be filled with coins."

We cross the street for the ice cream shop and I order three scoops of bubble gum in a waffle cone. As we walk the streets with our cones, thoughts of my parents' money problems and my anger at Rudy fade into the distance. I spend most of my time scanning the ground for coins.

By the time we're on our way back to the car, my feet ache but my pockets jingle with the sound of money. I haven't counted it yet, but I have a feeling I've won the bet.

And I've added to my collection for Mom and Dad.

At Grandpa's house, I dump the coins onto the kitchen table while Grandpa makes dinner and Alex sits across from me with a frown on his face.

Just to make him suffer a little, I take my time counting the coins. "Seven pennies." One by one I drop them onto the table. "Two dimes and one quarter."

"Humph." Alex looks away from my pile of coins.

"I think that makes 52 cents." I smile at him, pick up the coins, and then let them clink back on top of each other. The sweet sound of success!

"Fine. You win," he says. "I'll do your chores tonight." Alex drops his head into his hands and moans.

I smile. No chores and more money for Mom and Dad. Fifty-two cents isn't much, but every cent counts.

The smell of garlic and butter make my stomach growl. "What's for dinner, Grandpa?" I ask.

Grandpa wipes his hands on a towel and stands

next me. "Just spaghetti and garlic bread." He leans over and picks up one of my pennies. He holds it up to the light and turns it over. "Hmm."

"What's wrong?" I ask.

He rubs his chin and raises an eyebrow. Something he always does when he's thinking hard. "You've got yourself a

peculiar coin here."

Chapter 14
Penny Power

After I scarf down my spaghetti, leaving a pool of sauce above my lip, I wipe with my sleeve, drain my milk and smack my cup back on the table.

"Done."

Grandpa laughs. "I guess so."

I push my dishes aside and get up. "Can we look on the Internet to find out about my coin now?" I'm ready to get the scoop on this "PECULIAR" penny, already having lost interest in the coins I brought from home.

I still don't know what Grandpa means by "peculiar" but, in my mind, it sounds a little like "worth money." And extra money right now could help solve a lot of problems for our family.

"I want to see too," Alex says and twists spaghetti around his fork until the metal disappears. He opens his mouth wide and pushes it in, looking a lot like a chipmunk.

The image of Alex's head with a chipmunk body makes me laugh. I use a finger to scratch the top of his head. Using my most irritating kiddie voice I tell him, "Little chipmunk has to do the dishes, remember?"

"STARP!" Alex just about spits the spaghetti right out of his mouth telling me to stop. He swats at my hand like I'm a fly in July.

"You made a deal, Alex," Grandpa says. He

stands and gives me a warning look. Then he goes to the living room and comes back with his laptop. He sets it in front of me. Out of his pocket, he pulls a penny in a clear plastic cover and places it next to the computer.

"Where's your penny?" he asks.

I take Peculiar Penny from my pocket and put it alongside his coin.

"Take a look," Grandpa says.

I pick up his coin and study it. Then I pick up mine and do the same. "What am I supposed to be looking for?"

"Let's look again." Grandpa puts on his reading glasses and holds both coins up to the light. "Yep. Just what I thought."

He stares at them without saying anything more.

"What?" I shout, pounding the table. "What is

it?"

Grandpa laughs and puts both coins in front of me again. "Take your time. Look at the front of them," he says. "What do you notice?"

I place my head at table level and study them. "They're just two pennies."

"Keep looking."

I squint to get a clearer image. They were both minted in 1960 and have a "D" for the Denver mint.

After spending another minute without anything coming to mind, I give up. "They're exactly the same Grandpa," I say. "The only difference is that the 1960 D on your coin is printed kind of weird. But mine isn't."

Grandpa gives me a round of applause.

"So, he figured it out?" Alex asks through a mouthful of garlic bread.

"Yep!" Grandpa says.

"I did?"

I look at the coins again. What did I figure out? The writing on the coins is different. So what?

Grandpa looks at me like I should know.

"Can't you just tell me?" I put my head in my hands. "My brain is getting tired."

He laughs. "Alright." He picks up his coin. "Like you said, my coin is a bit different."

He points to the date on his penny. "If you look real close you'll see that the date was actually printed twice, one on top of the other," he says. "The first time they struck the coin they used larger print. The second time it was smaller."

I blink hard a few times and try to focus. "Yeah. Yours is kind of blurry looking. And I can see an extra D."

"Right." He grabs my penny. "Your coin doesn't have that problem."

His coin catches a glint of light in his hand. It makes me want to reach out, grab it and stuff it in my pocket.

Grandpa interrupts my thoughts. "But, it's probably worth something."

Worth something? That's exactly what I wanted to hear. It's enough to get my heart pumping and lifts me out of my chair, beating my fist in the air. "Yes!"

Finally finished eating, Alex moseys to the sink with his plate. "How much could he get for it?"

"Well, that's why we have the computer." Grandpa clicks a button and the screen lights up.

While I wait on his Internet search and the good news, I relish watching Alex wash the dishes. By the time he's finished, he has beads of sweat dotting his forehead. He looks like an

Eskimo on a hot day.

"That's it," he says with a long breath. He rolls his sleeves down and falls into a chair exhausted.

Grandpa looks up from the computer and scans the kitchen. "Nice work, Alex."

Still breathless, he lets out a weak, "Thanks." He looks at me. "No more bets, I promise."

115

I laugh. "I bet you won't keep that promise!"

"Here we go," Grandpa says and turns the computer in my direction. Ebay is on the screen. Pictures of pennies line the left side.

"Now, this isn't the best way to find out what it's worth, but it looks like yours is selling for about $2, Jake." He pats me on the back with congratulations.

$2? Peculiar Penny is only worth $2?

Shocked by how little it's worth, I can't help but frown and stare at the floor.

Grandpa taps the screen. "That's not enough for you?" His voice sounds tense.

I look at the Ebay list with prices and pictures and "Buy it Now" tabs next to them. "Are you sure it's not worth more?"

I click the down arrow and scan the screen

farther. Listed are 1960D pennies with large dates or small dates. I look at my coin again, which looks like it has a date that was printed small. Some small date coins are selling for $10. At the bottom of the screen I find a "small date" penny for sale for $25.

"Why are these all worth more?" I ask.

Grandpa pushes his seat away from the table and takes off his reading glasses. "Your coin is a bit scratched up." He points to the computer. "Most of these coins are uncirculated. They've never been used or even touched."

I cram my lips together in frustration and click to the next page. My eyes almost pop out of my head when I see a coin listed for $350.

"Whoa! Look at this one." I enlarge the picture.

The coin is just like Grandpa's.

I read through the description. "Yours is a double small date/large date, right?"

"Yep."

I can hardly believe what I'm seeing. "Do you know how much it's worth?"

"Yes. I know," Grandpa says, as calm as can be.

I spin my head in his direction. An image pops into my mind: I see Dad hunched over the job ads and Mom's eyes red from crying.

$350 could change things.

Finally feeling a little bit of hope, I clutch Grandpa's coin in my hand and ask,

"Can I have it?"

Chapter 15
The "Real Thing" Rules

Grandpa stares at me a minute, grabs the coin and then sticks it in his pocket. "Nope," he says. "This one's not for you. At least, not right now."

My throat tightens as Grandpa's face grows serious. "Sit down," he says.

I drop back into my seat, feeling a growing tension in my chest. Alex sits too and watches us with a silly look of curiosity that I feel like wiping off his face. Instead, I grit my teeth and keep quiet.

Grandpa slides back in his chair. "You can have the coin, Jake …"

My heart takes a leap.

"… when you grow up."

That heart-leap turns into a belly flop.

Grandpa folds his hands in front of him. "It's for your future."

I don't hear much of what he says after that. The tension I'd been feeling is now a full-grown rock sitting on my chest. I hear something about the coin paying for my college books and I gnash my teeth until my jaw starts to ache.

Doesn't Grandpa understand? Doesn't he get it? I don't need to go to college! I'd rather use the money to eat or maybe we could actually keep our house.

But I don't tell Grandpa that. My mouth stays shut and I take off to the guest room as soon as he lets me go. Running out of there is the only way to hide the growing lump in my throat that can only mean one thing …

Tears are on their way.

Once I'm in bed, I can't hold them back any longer. Then the tears, a lumpy mattress and the thought of a penny worth $350 keep me awake.

Dad has been out of work for more than a month and I'm supposed to wait for Grandpa's penny until I go to college?

I pound the mattress in anger and I hear the door knob jiggle. I stiffen at the sound until I hear Alex moving around the room getting ready for bed.

I shift toward the wall and sling a blanket over my head, biting my lip to hold back the tears. I don't know how long I wait, but once I know Alex is asleep by his thick, heavy breaths, I slide out of bed and go to the couch. I grab the fluffy blanket off the edge and hide, thinking about all of the possible consequences of moving.

The tears I'd been choking back return with a vengeance. Trying to fix it all has become too much work. I'm deep in the midst of my pity party with my head under the covers when I hear a noise that causes a shiver to run up my spine. I throw the blankets back to see where it came from.

Grandpa stands over me. "You alright, Jake?"

Wanting to hide my tears, I bury my face in the arm of the couch. "Forget about it. It's okay."

The cushions next to me sink as Grandpa sits down. "What's going on?" He puts his arm around me.

Heaving a big sigh, I sit up. Moonlight shines through the curtains and brightens Grandpa's face.

He looks worried.

"I just need that coin, that's all."

He narrows his eyes. "What for?"

I'm starting to wonder if he even knows about Dad's layoff. I lean back and stare into the dark. "Dad's been out of work for over a month now. We need money."

Grandpa squeezes my shoulder. "I know. And your dad and mom are taking care of things. You don't have to worry."

How could he be so wrong? I shake my head. "I do have to worry. I mean, I can't move to some state that no one has ever heard of. I just can't."

I tug the blanket and get off the couch, pacing. After several passes back and forth, the blanket knocks some pictures off the coffee table and they crash to the floor.

I try to read Grandpa's expression. But there's nothing. He just gets up and goes into the kitchen. When he doesn't come back right away, I reset the pictures and check for broken glass. Happy there isn't any, I pull my shaky legs to my chest, wrap my arms around them and wait.

A few minutes later, Grandpa returns with two steaming cups of hot cocoa topped with whipped cream.

"Here you go." He hands me a cup and switches on a lamp as he sits down. He looks straight into my eyes. "Do you know what the Bible says about God taking care of us?"

I clench my jaw and blow air out my nose. The cup in my hand jiggles so I set it down and start pacing again. "I don't know, Grandpa." I turn to face him. "Why can't you just give me that coin? I'll sell it and give the money to Mom and Dad."

Grandpa frowns. "Humor this old man for a minute. Okay?" He pats the couch next to him. "Sit down. Tell me what you think about my question."

"The Bible? God taking care of us?" I suck the whipped cream off the top of the hot chocolate. "I'm not sure."

My leg bobs up and down again.

Then a picture pops into my mind. "I know this sounds crazy, but I picture him kind of like Batman. Batman rescues everyone. I imagine God's kind of like that."

It's not much, but it's the only thing I can think of.

"Well …"

"I mean, God's our hero. Right?" I shrug and wait, leg dangerously close to causing another crash.

"Uh, kind of." Grandpa scratches his forehead and frowns again. He puts down his cocoa and moves to the bookshelf. It's stuffed with so many books, it looks like it might spit a few out any second.

He points to one of the rows. "Cartoons are fun but let's look at the real thing to find out exactly what He says."

I cock my head. "The real thing?"

He pulls a fat Bible off the shelf.

"The Real Thing," he says as he holds it up.

He opens it and a bunch old church bulletins fall out. It looks like the pages might come out too. "How are you ever going to know when someone tells you the wrong thing about God if you don't know what The Real Thing says?"

"Huh?"

Grandpa flips through his Real Thing and finds what he's looking for.

He grabs his glasses, clears his throat and reads aloud. "That is why I tell you not to worry about everyday life," he runs a finger under the words as he reads, "whether you have enough food and drink, or enough clothes to wear." He stops for a second and looks up at me.

I shrug again and he keeps reading. "Look at the birds. They don't plant or harvest or store food in barns, for your heavenly Father feeds them.

And aren't you far more valuable to him than they are?"

Grandpa closes his Bible and sets it on the table. "That's from Matthew, Chapter 6. What does it mean?"

I fiddle with the strings on the end of the blanket and sigh. "I think it means that I shouldn't worry so much."

"Exactly." Grandpa taps me on the shoulder and gives me a big smile.

I struggle to break my frown. "But somebody's got to do something. I can't just sit around like a little bird and wait for someone to drop worms from the sky."

Grandpa gets into his thinking position, one eyebrow up and a hand on his chin. "That's not your job, Jake. It's God's and your parents'."

It sure feels like it's my job. I bite my lip and focus on the coffee table. The fat Bible stares up at me. "Why do you call your Bible 'The Real Thing'?"

Grandpa picks it up and rubs it like it's his favorite stuffed animal. "This is the truth." He sets it in my lap. "There are lots of lies out there, tons of fakes. But you'll always find the truth in here."

I stare at Grandpa's Bible for a minute. I let my hand fall onto it, rubbing it and thinking about the little birds and how God takes care of them.

Maybe God really would take care of us, too.

I take a deep breath and notice my leg has stopped shaking. For a minute I feel at peace. But Dad's face enters my mind and the feeling disappears.

No matter what the Bible says, Dad still doesn't have a job.

My leg goes to work again. If God is taking care of our family, why is Dad still sitting at home

Scouring the Internet for Jobs?

Chapter 16
Itching for Ideas

The hour and a half drive home from Grandpa's house on Sunday night gives me too much time to think. Money problems and Rudy's face cloud my mind. I check my phone more than once, hoping I might have missed a call, but there's nothing. I also spend my time trying to come up with a new money making idea. But I have nothing there either. The emptiness of it all feels heavy.

As soon as we pull into my driveway, I hug Grandpa and dash into the house, waving to Mom and Dad as I take off for my room. Wally chases me and sneaks in behind me just as I close the door. I give him a little pat and drop onto my bed.

Tears burn my eyes again with the uncertainty of everything. I try to shake them away and I hear a knock.

"It's Mom. Can I come in?"

I clear my throat and cram my palms into my eyes. "Yeah."

She opens the door and the sound of Alex abusing his harmonica floats in with her. "You ran by so fast, I didn't even get to see how your weekend went."

I'm glad when she closes the door behind her and shuts out Alex's so-called music. She sits down next to me.

"It was good." I keep my head down so she won't notice any leftover tears.

"Grandpa said you found a cool coin." She dips her head trying to look at my face but I turn away.

"Yeah. It's cool."

"Can I see it?"

I take a deep breath and pretend to look around my room. "I'm not sure where I put it. Can I show you some other time?"

"Sure." She puts her arm around my shoulder and squeezes. "Glad you two are home." She sits a minute more and then moves toward the door.

It's a relief to know that she's on her way out, but I stop her anyway. "Um ... any more job news?"

Her happy grin changes to a frown. Right away I regret asking. "Nothing. No interviews lined up for this week." She pastes the smile back on. "Just keep praying. Everything will be okay."

I put on my fake smile, too. "Sure, Mom."

She places a hand on the door. "Dinner will be ready in fifteen minutes."

As she leaves the room, I drop my clownish grin. With a sigh, I throw myself back on the bed and continue brainstorming money ideas.

The "do not worry" sermon Grandpa gave me passes through my mind. It seems so easy for him to pick up the Bible and know what to do. But no matter how long I search for answers

I can't find one.

I spot my Bible on my desk and grab it. I guess it couldn't hurt to take a look at THE REAL THING, as Grandpa says.

I thumb through it but I have no idea where to start. Finally, I close my eyes and let the Bible fall onto my bed. I spin my finger over the Bible then slip it into a random page.

When I open my eyes, I'm staring at Chapter 28 in the book of First Samuel. I pick it up and read. The further I get into it, the weirder it sounds. A guy named Saul visits a fortune-teller in Endor and asks her to conjure up a dead guy for him to talk to.

I drop The Real Thing onto my bed and let my jaw hang open. So, this is the help I get?

Am I supposed to talk to a fortune-teller? Or a dead guy?

I look up at my ceiling, hoping for an answer.

"What about Endor?" I ask the ceiling. The only Endor I know is the land of the Ewoks from the *Star Wars* movies.

Maybe it's a sign to sell my Ewok action figures?

After a while, my brain hurts. I close the Bible with a thud and put it back on the desk.

Did I really think I'd get answers with my eyes closed and a spinning finger?

I fling myself onto the bed and notice an old soda can sitting on my bedside table. I pick it up and jiggle. A little Coke sloshes in the bottom and I take the last swig. It's a little warm, but still tasty.

I crumple the can and eye my metal trash bin. I fling the can into the air and sink a basket. It clinks against other cans and the idea I'd spent the last few hours looking for finally reveals itself.

RECYCLING!

Why didn't I think of it before? It's easy and there's a never-ending supply of cans and bottles at any park. And with Ben's help, the money would come rolling in. If Ben's willing to help, that is.

I grab the phone and punch in Ben's number. "God gave me an idea."

"Uh ... hello?"

It's Ben's mom. "Sorry, Mrs. Dorson. Uh, can I talk to Ben?"

Mrs. Dorson laughs and I hear her set the phone down. I drum my fingers on my desk while I wait.

"Hello?"

"God gave me an idea!"

I blurt it out again, hoping that's enough to break the tension since Ben and I haven't talked in a few days.

"Hello to you, too."

"Oh, yeah. Hi." I swallow a growing lump in my throat. "God gave me an idea. I need your help," I tell him.

Silence.

"Ben?"

More silence. Then rustling of papers.

"Not sure I'm ready for another one of your big ideas." Ben's voice sounds doubtful. "Besides, I haven't heard from you in a few days. How's Rudy?"

I squirm a little. "Uh, I don't know. Haven't talked to him." I change the topic in hopes he'll forget about Rudy. "This will be fun. An adventure." I bite my lip and wait for his answer, trying to convince myself as well as him.

"Maybe you should tell me what it is," he says.

"Oh, yeah." I sit on my floor with my back to the wall. "I want to recycle."

There's no response from Ben at first and then there's laughter. "That's it? You want to recycle?" A few snickers. "So, going green is your big idea?" He clears his throat and finally stops laughing. "Sure, I can help. I've been keeping newspapers on the back porch for my Dad. Come on over and get them."

It's not the response I was looking for but at least he's willing to help. "Listen. Haven't you ever taken a bunch of cans to one of those recycling places? You can earn good money that way."

"You're still trying to earn money to help your family?" Ben pauses. "You know you probably don't have to do that. You worry too much."

I stare at my floor and then at Wally curled up on

my bed. He doesn't have a care in the world. No matter what happens, he knows he'll have a roof over his head and food in his bowl. Somehow he has faith that I'll take care of him.

"So, will you help me or not?" I say, a little irritated.

Silence again.

Ben takes a deep breath and lets it out into the phone. "Sure. I'll help you. What do I need to do?"

"Just meet me in front of the school tomorrow when the last bell rings. Make sure you ride your bike."

I click the phone off then slide onto the bed next to Wally. I make a mental list of all the nearby parks. I fall asleep praying I won't have to fight any of the local street people for the cans and that Ben will

get off my case about Rudy for a while.

Chapter 17
Hungry for the Hunt

The hunt for cans and bottles starts at the preschool playground at Balboa Park. Perched on my bike, I inhale the salty smell of the bay in the wind.

When I take a look around, I find a couple of mommies eyeing Ben and me. One of them keeps switching her gaze from me to her kid, then from her kid to me. I feel a bit like a criminal so I try to look younger by slumping my shoulders. I give Ms. Suspicious a shy smile and wave. She frowns, grabs her kid by the hand and fast-walks away.

My jaw hangs open and I poke Ben in the side to get his attention. But he's looking in the opposite direction shaking his head and he misses the entire thing. When he finally turns around, he pulls off his glasses and rubs them on his shirt. "Not a can or bottle in sight. Are you sure about this?"

I glance back in the direction where Ms. Suspicious ran off and shrug. "We just have to do some reconnaissance." I pull two large, black garbage bags from my backpack and fling one in Ben's direction. "You know, do a little hunting." Ben catches the bag. "Tie this onto your handle bars and follow me."

I attach my bag to the front of my bike and take off down the trail that leads to the baseball fields. When I look behind me, Ben's still trying to tie on his bag. My bag, on the other hand, is filling with air.

I figure Ben will catch up, so I hit the pedals even harder. The faster I go, the bigger the bag grows. By the time I reach the baseball field, it looks like a miniature hot-air balloon and my bike has become a whole lot harder to balance.

But it's a challenge I can't pass up.

I stand and pedal harder for more power. When I turn the bend near first base I realize I'm at the top of a hill and there's no stopping.

With my legs screaming in pain, back tight and mouth open, I fly down the hill with the bag beating against my body.

I throw my arms in the air and coast down the steep incline.

Just as I'm at the peak of the thrill,

the bag explodes!

I'm starting to think that I'm an explosion magnet. This one sounds like a bottle rocket and feels like one too. The force of the blast sends my bike and me flying off the path. The wheel hits a rock and the bike goes one way and I go the other. I land on my back in the grass with a THUD.

When I open my eyes, Ben's standing over me. His mouth is in a twisted frown and his eyes are wide. I've never seen him look so scared.

I lie there a minute staring at him, thinking that maybe I should fake being paralyzed to panic him even more.

When he doesn't say anything, I figure I've already scared him speechless. So I jump up.

"Were you worried about me?" I say in a baby voice.

Ben lowers his eyebrows and gives me a mad look.

"But that was …" I pause for effect and stare Ben right in the eye, "… awesome!"

Ben throws himself to the ground. "Arrggggg! Why do you always do this kind of thing to me?"

A chuckle bursts from my throat, out of my control. Before I know it, I'm doubled over with laughter. Ben's face stays mad for a minute but he finally joins in. I sit down next to him and he socks me in the arm.

"That did look pretty cool," he finally says.

"Yeah. It was like my bike became a rocket and the bag was the jet fuel."

"You should have seen yourself." Ben waves his arms in the air and whines like a girl. "Eeeeeehhhh! You looked like my little sister on the merry-go-round at school."

I give him a push and hop up. "Whatever." I look myself up and down. There are grass stains on my knees and a rip in my shirt. I shrug. "Come on. Let's go find some stuff to recycle."

"I still don't see anything." He motions to the baseball field and the picnic area near where I fell.

I check the area and there's nothing in sight. "That means we'll have to go to Plan B." Money's out there waiting for Mom and Dad and it's my job to find it. "We're going to have to look in the trash cans," I say.

Ben falls back into the grass. "You've got to be kidding me.

"I told you, it's an adventure. Who knows what we'll find. Let's go." I pick up my bike and look it over. It can still be ridden but it's a little scratched up and wobbly. I hope Dad won't notice.

More important though, the bottom of my plastic bag is completely blown out. "You've got the only bag," I tell him.

"Grrrrrr." It's Ben's only comment to me as he

gets up and goes for his bike. He leads the way to the nearest picnic table and trash can. "You first," he says.

Several tall trees with droopy limbs surround the area and only a few people are in sight. I set my bike down and peek inside the can. It smells like the end of the world, but it's full and I don't see even one can or bottle. Digging would be the next step.

I lean into the can and start to move things around. The first item I pick up looks like a half-eaten ice cream sandwich with the ice cream melted away. I toss it on the ground and pull out a bunch of newspapers.

Under the papers, two empty soda cans wait for me. "Gotcha!" I grab them both and hand them to Ben.

Once I find these, I have hope. I tear into that container like it's

a box of donuts on Sunday.

Flinging the trash onto the ground, I search until I have five bottles and eight more cans.

We put them in Ben's bag, stuff the trash back inside the barrel and set off for the next one.

We cover the west side of the park, avoiding another kiddie playground. I dumpster-dive at the picnic areas and Ben carries the loot. We fill his bag within the first half hour. I find two more bags in one of the trash bins and attach them to my bike.

No more rocket rides though. I need to keep my

bike in one piece. And, besides, this is serious. Money making at its best.

By the time we get the east side, my back aches from the crash and the constant leaning into trash cans. "Could you search for a while?" I ask Ben and plop down onto the bench at a wooden picnic table.

His eyes grow wide again. "Uh-uh. No way."

"Please man. My back hurts. I think I might have really injured something in that wreck." I hold my back and wince a little to make my point. Just as I lean against the table, a sliver of wood sticks through my jeans and sinks into the skin of my behind.

I let out a yelp, hopping off the bench quicker than a

gymnast at a trampoline park.

Ben stares at me.

I rub my backside and groan, hoping to soothe the pain a little. But the sliver of wood is stuck in my pants and catches on my hand. Pain shoots up my arm.

"Ouch!" I stick my finger in my mouth.

"Okay. You don't have to fake being hurt. I'll do it," he says.

"But–"

"It's just because you're my best friend." Ben yanks one of the bags from my hand and stomps over to a barrel. Before I can say anything, he fills the bag and heads for another nearby can.

With my finger still in my mouth, I pull the wood out of my pants. Despite the fact that I'm still in pain, watching Ben at work makes me feel a lot better. I could have explained myself to him, but decide not to. Instead, I just rub away the sting in my backside and follow him. Within ten minutes, Ben's other bag is full and the sliver of wood is a distant memory.

"Okay. I'm done. Let's go home," he says.

"We still have more containers to search." I see at least three cans at the top of the hill where my rocket ride started.

Ben raises his eyebrows. "We don't have any more bags. Can't you see that?"

"I bet I can find another bag. If I do, will you search the last three containers for me?"

Another long pause from Ben. He scratches his head, closes his eyes. "Alright. But only if you find another bag," he says.

"Yes! You're awesome. I'll be right back." I hop on my bike and ride wobbling toward the baseball field.

Before I even made the offer to Ben, I'd already spied a bag stuck on the chain-link backstop. I pull it off and check for holes. It's perfect. By the time I get back to Ben, I can tell by his frown that he regrets the deal.

"Here you go." I hand it to him.

He grits his teeth and takes it. "Let's get this over with. I smell like old soda and

We ride up the hill and Ben goes to work on the trash bins. He pulls half a bag of recyclables from the first two. The last can is piled high with dirty paper plates and cups. Ben digs his hands in and pushes them aside to get to what's underneath.

As the paper goods move, Ben lets out a scream louder than a howler monkey. He jumps back, yanking his hand out, and it's

dripping with blood.

Chapter 18
Back-up Plan Blues

"Whoa, what happened?" I let my bike drop and run to Ben.

He shakes his hand so fast that blood flies everywhere. But I can't see what's hurt.

I hold him by the shoulders and try to look him in the eye. "Stop moving."

Still in shock, he stares at his hand. I do too. Stuck right in its side is a piece of dark glass.

Ben may be a pretty tough guy, but he's never been able to stomach the sight of blood. His eyes go glassy and he looks like he's about to faint.

I gulp with the realization that it's probably my job to remove the glass. I tense my muscles and grab his arm. With one quick motion, I pinch the glass and pull it out. Ben doesn't say a word but his face turns pasty white.

I toss the glass back in the trash bin and take a closer look at the injury. Now that the glass is gone, the blood trickles out a bit slower and the cut doesn't look as bad. The shard was about an inch wide at the top. But the bottom turned into a little tip and that's all that went into Ben's skin. I shake Ben a little and lift his hand in front of his face.

"Look. It's not that bad. It's just a little hole," I tell him.

Ben blinks. "A little hole? That's what you call being harpooned by one of your stinking

RECYCLABLES?

"Well, we could call an ambulance." I laugh.

Ben frowns and looks at his hand. He squeezes the spot where the glass had been. A few more drops of blood spill out but the flow is slow.

He twists his mouth and then lets it turn into a smile. "Maybe we should call an ambulance for YOU. To take you to the crazy house."

He shakes out his hand and gets on his bike, leaving the bag of recyclables on the ground. "Let's go home."

Relieved that he's okay, I grab the bag and tie it to the handlebars with the other three. Then I follow Ben back to his house.

When we arrive, he leaves me in the garage with the cat smell and goes inside to get a Band-Aid. I empty all four bags on a mat and separate glass, plastic and aluminum. By the time I finish with the three healthy looking piles, Ben still hasn't come back.

I open the door to the house and call to him, "Hey, let's take this stuff over to the drop-off place. I'm ready to get some money."

"Can't you just go alone," he calls back.

I stand with the door open and look back at the piles. "The stuff is pretty heavy," I yell. "A little help?"

I hear a loud sigh. "I'm coming."

I sit on the floor next to my piles and begin stuffing the bottles and cans back into bags. I tie them off and hook one to each of my handlebars. Ben comes back out with an ace bandage tied around his hand. It's so thick, his hand looks like it got stuck in a baseball.

"Wow!" I give him a shocked look. "That's a pretty big Band-Aid."

"If you expect me to ride with those bags hanging from my bike, I need some protection." He holds his hand against his chest like he's cradling a baby.

I shake my head, attach the other two bags to his bike and hop on mine. I motion for him to follow. We ride down the hill to the recycling drop-off near the corner supermarket.

My heart stops when I pull up in front of the shack. The door is closed with a big sign that reads,

"Open Weekends Only."

I look at Ben and fling my head back. "Noooooo," I scream at the sky. "All that work and I have to wait until the weekend?"

"So I have to ride back up that hill with these bags still tied to my handlebars?" Ben asks.

I cringe. "Uh, how's the hand doing?"

He shrugs a little and doesn't say anything for about 1,000 seconds. Then he holds up his hand. "I guess it's okay. No big deal. I'll come back with you on Saturday."

"Really?"

"Yep. Let's go." He starts pedaling back to his

house. I watch him ride up the hill for a minute then follow.

On the way home, I come up with a back-up plan. Plan C. I repeat my new motto in my head: No giving up. Help Mom and Dad.

I pitch Plan C to Ben over a cup of lemonade in his kitchen.

Ben's jaw tenses when he hears what I've come up with. "So, you're going to call as many people as you can and talk them into letting you pick up their recycling?"

"Yeah, I bet we could be done in two hours if we time it right."

"We?" Ben rubs his forehead and doesn't look at me. "If you can get somebody to give you their recycling, I'm in." He laughs. "I wouldn't miss that for the world."

As soon as Ben gives me the go-ahead, I pull out my phone and start punching numbers. After fifteen minutes, I have just two guys whose parents are willing to give me their stuff. I wrack my brain for more names. Then I remember there's one person I haven't called. Rudy. It's a risk. But it gives me a reason to call him back, since he hasn't called me.

Without letting Ben know, I make the call. "Hey, it's me, Jake," I say into the phone.

"Jake who?"

I look at Ben, then turn my back to him and whisper into the phone. "You know, Jake from the history project."

"Oh … uh … yeah. Sorry. What's up?"

"Um, well …" I've suddenly forgotten why I called. Ben clears his throat from behind me. When I turn around, he's pointing at his cut finger.

I nod and give him a weak smile. "I'm recycling." Now it sounds a little dorkier than I thought it would. "I'll take your stuff to the drop-off if you let me keep the money."

A long pause.

"I guess. I think we have a bag of cans in the garage. Are you going to come over and get them?"

"Yeah. Thanks, Rudy. We could do it right now if you want." I turn back around and give Ben a thumbs up. He frowns.

"Okay. I guess I'll see you soon," Rudy says.

I click the phone off and look at Ben. He's still frowning. "What's wrong?" I ask despite knowing exactly why he's upset.

"You know what I think about that Rudy guy." He shuffles around the kitchen putting our cups in the sink and stacking newspapers.

"He's giving us his stuff. If you ask me, that's pretty cool of him?" It's both a statement and a question. If Rudy was such a bad guy, would he have agreed to help me out?

I pat Ben on the back and squeeze his shoulder. "Come on. Let's get going. I need to be home before dark."

Ben gives me an angry look but follows me to gather the recyclables. Our first stop is

Rudy's house.

Ben stays on his bike at the sidewalk, refusing to come to the door. I stand on the porch and hit the buzzer. Rudy appears with the bag in his hands. He pushes the screen door open and steps out. As he closes the door behind him, I hear a bunch of voices inside.

"Here. It's all we have." He shoves the bag at me.

"Uh, thanks."

Rudy looks back toward the house, shifting on his feet. "Hey, I was gonna call you. Do you think you could help me study for the history test that's coming up next week?"

I look back at Ben. He's straddling his bike and has his arms tight across his chest. He eyes Rudy with

a Stone-cold Stare.

"Next week?" I tap a fist against my thigh, not knowing what to think.

"Help a friend out?" he asks, staring at me with innocent eyes and a look of expectation.

A friend? I give in. "Uh. Sure. Why not?"

"Great. Let's start Wednesday night." He opens the door and the sound of the voices drifts out again. "I gotta go. Talk to you later."

Before I can even thank him for the cans or say anything about our tutoring session, he shuts the door. As I turn to walk back to my bike, I hear a thunder of laughter come from inside. I can tell Ben hears it, too. He looks at the house with disbelief.

I chuckle. "I wonder what that's all about." I slide the bag onto my bike. "Ready?"

"What were you talking to Rudy about for so long? I thought we just came to get the cans."

I try not to look Ben in the eye. "I told him I would help him study for the history test," I whisper.

"You what?" Ben's eyes shoot darts my way.

"No big deal, just a little time on Wednesday night." The minute I say "Wed ..." I know I'm in trouble.

"Just Wednesday night? What happened to church? What happened to hanging out with me?" Ben's eyes turn into slants.

"It's just this time. You know, a little help for a friend. He helped me out." I point to the bag. "So I'm returning the favor."

"Don't you get it, Jake?" Ben shakes his head. "That guy is not your friend. He just wants help from you because you're the class history nerd. After that, he'll never talk to you again."

Ben's words make me flinch. "I … I don't think so," I stammer.

"Really?" Ben starts to pedal away. As I watch his back I hear,

"Then enjoy your new friend."

Chapter 19
Bathroom Brawl?

At school the next day, I follow Ben to his classes because he refuses to talk to me. When he walks by the bathroom before second period, he turns around and I'm tempted to hide in the bushes because I feel like a stalker. On the way to lunch, I get so close he can probably smell me. But this time he doesn't turn around, he doesn't leave an empty seat for me and never says a word.

By the time our history class starts, my heart is in my throat and I'm feeling pretty rejected. When I sit at my desk, I wave to him and he just gives me a weak smile. His smile turns upside down when Rudy approaches me.

"Wednesday, right?" Rudy asks. But his voice is so quiet I can barely hear him.

I look around, wondering why he's whispering. "Yeah," I say, noticing Ben watching.

Rudy looks around too. "Cool," he whispers and walks to the back of the room and slides into his desk.

I watch Rudy a minute. He high-fives another guy and makes a joke about our history teacher, Mr. Birgdon. For some reason, his whispering problem is suddenly cured. I turn my attention back to Ben and he also has his eyes on Rudy and a look of disgust on his face.

I get out of my seat to see if Ben will finally talk to

me but, just as I do, Mr. Birgdon walks in and I freeze.

"Time to get started everyone." Taller than most of the basketball players on the high school team and a little scary looking with a heavy, dark beard, I decide that sitting is the best idea. My confusion about Rudy's whispers and questions about Ben's attitude would

have to wait.

Mr. Birgdon picks up a dry erase marker and writes on the board:

- What year did WWII start?
- Who were the main players in the war?
- What were the major effects of the war on the US economy?

"Today we're going to practice our research skills," he says. "Grab a partner and use the various books in the room to find the answers to these questions."

I re-read the questions. The first two are easy to answer without doing research. The last one is going to take a little time. But that's not what worries me the most.

My biggest problem is going to be finding a partner. Ben, my usual choice, is unlikely to work out. Just in case, I turn in my chair to look his way and find him standing right in front of me with a pen and paper in his hand.

"Ready?" he says.

For a second, my voice is gone. "Uh, yeah." I

can't help but let a smile rise.

Ben pushes his hair away from his glasses, taps his pencil on his arm and waits. For a long moment, I stare at him, not sure what to do. When he doesn't move, I finally pull an empty desk next to mine and bury my face in my book. "Where should we start?"

"You're the history nerd, you tell me," he says. His voice sounds a bit strained so I look up to check his face, expecting to see angry eyes. Instead, his usual cheesy smile is plastered there and again

I'm Speechless.

"Come on coin collector, let's do this." Ben laughs.

I'm not sure why, but he's gone from cold shoulder to friendly within a few minutes. But this unexpected attitude change is a relief. "Forgive me?" I squeak out.

He smirks and shrugs. "Yeah. No problem."

I clear my throat and feel the relief flood my body. "Well, I already know the answers to questions one and two." I blow on my knuckles and rub them on my chest, congratulating myself.

Ben chuckles and punches me in the arm. It hurts a little, but at least things are back to normal.

We spend the next twenty minutes researching question three. By the end of this time, we've finished our paragraph before anyone else in the class.

We hand the sheet to Mr. Birgdon. He looks over it and rubs his beard as we wait. The fact that he doesn't say anything at first makes me shift on my feet.

Ben and I look at each other and scratch our heads at the same time.

"You two have some interesting answers to question three." Mr. Birgdon shakes his head. "So, you think a major impact on the US economy was that lots of people moved to New Jersey?"

I let out a nervous laugh and look at Ben. "Uh, you didn't read the back." I point to the other side of the paper where I had finished my paragraph about New Jersey. Hopefully, Mr. Birgdon doesn't have questions about why I chose that particular state rather than somewhere else. Talking about my family's financial problems at school would be

worse than eating broccoli.

Mr. Birgdon turns over the paper and reads. He runs his fingers through his beard again. But this time he nods and smiles. "Hmmm." He smiles again. When he looks up, his eyes are big. "Right on, guys. I didn't follow your logic at first, but this is good."

Ben turns to me and holds up his hand for a high five. I smack it and pump my fist in the air. "I knew it! Wars always make people change jobs and move. And I'm sure some of them moved to New Jersey!"

Without warning, my brain makes a U-turn and I'm picturing me and Mike Winters in our snow boots again. I try to shake off the feeling of dread that comes with it.

Mr. Birgdon's laughter pulls me out of it. "Yes. I think that's a possibility," he says and hands the paper back to me and points to the rest of the class. "You have some free time while people finish up. Just make sure you're quiet."

Ben and I go back to our seats and play Sudoku together for the rest of the period. Every once in a while he rubs the Band-Aid on his hand where the glass had been stuck. I wince a little at the thought of

dripping blood

and yesterday's fears of a lost finger. Ben adds a number to the Sudoku and never says anything about it, or much of anything else.

Just as we are finishing a game, he finally speaks up. "By the way, I collected some more cans for you." He fills in another Sudoku square. "I went to my grandma's last night and she had three bags full."

"Really?" I shake my head in surprise. "That's awesome. Thanks." I pause and stare at him, wondering how he could be such a good guy. "You're a great friend," I tell him.

"No big deal." The bell rings and he slides the desk back to its spot. "I'll catch you later. You can come by and pick them up tonight if you want."

I watch Ben slip out the door as I stuff my papers into my backpack and get ready to head home. Before I leave campus, I make a pit-stop at the bathroom.

I'm more than ready to get home after a long day, but while washing my hands, I notice a penny on the floor between the wall and the trash can. I dry off and reach for it but it's too far inside the little crevice. An opening behind the can leaves a perfect space for me, so I go around and try again.

I end up lying on the ground behind the can. This time I slide my hand into the space and I'm able to touch the penny. I tap it with the tip of my finger and the edge lifts. Just as I pick it up, I hear my name.

"Jake King?"

I'm about to stand up, but stop myself when I hear the rest of the conversation.

"What are you doing talking to that loser?"

I don't recognize the voice. It alternates between sounding high like Dora the Explorer and kind of deep and angry like Darth Vader. I stay in my spot, hidden behind the trash can with blood rushing to my face and feeling the heat of both fear and anger.

"Nothin'. I just talked him into helping me with a history project. Now he's going to help me ace the test next week." It's Rudy's voice.

"So, are you friends with him now or something?" asks the guy with the Dora-Vader voice.

"Of course not. I wouldn't be caught dead hanging around with someone like him," Rudy says.

I hear water running and try to scrunch up my body so they won't see me. If they find me listening,

I might as well be dead.

They'd likely pound me to the ground right there in the middle of the bathroom. And no one would ever know ... they probably wouldn't find my body for days.

The sound of another faucet being turned on catches my attention and makes me regain focus, taking my mind off these terrifying thoughts.

To make sure I'm safe, hiding is my best chance. But, I'm so close to the sinks, I don't know if I'll be able to avoid being found out.

As Rudy's voice seems to be getting nearer and nearer to my position, my leg jitters reach an all-time record. I hold my breath.

"He's just a free ride to an A," I hear Rudy say.

"I hope so," says Dora-Vader.

The water turns off and, just as quickly as they came, the sound of footsteps fades away and then disappears. Hoping they don't plan to come back, I let the tension fall from my muscles and lean back against the wall.

I look over the penny and give it a kiss. If it weren't for that coin, I never would have heard their conversation. It might have even saved my life.

After a minute of collecting myself, I begin to think through everything I heard. I can't believe what Rudy said about me. It makes my blood boil and I pound my fist on the trash can. The crashing sound echoes through the bathroom and pain shoots through my hand.

I pull myself up off the floor. My face looks back at me in the mirror. The frown I see looks like someone pulled two strings connected to my lips and tied them to my **toes.**

Chapter 20
Expecting Explanations

Wednesday night comes and I pick up the phone to cancel my tutoring session with Rudy. There's no way I could meet with him after the Bathroom Incident.

"Hi, Rudy. It's me, Jake."

"Hey! What's up, man?" For some reason, he sounds happy to hear from me.

"Um, I can't tutor you tonight," I tell him, tapping my fingers on my desk and trying to hold back from saying all of the other not-too-nice things I'd thought about.

"Really?" He pauses. "Too bad. It was going to be fun hanging out with you again."

I stop my tapping. "Oh." I can't seem to find any words. "Um ... we were just going to study history."

"I know," says Rudy. "I just had a blast last time we were at your house."

I get up and pace around my room. Suddenly, all of those angry words I wanted to say are gone. I kick a few old toys out of my way. "You did?"

"Yeah. But maybe we can study some other time?"

Confusion sets in. I picture myself on the floor of the bathroom behind the trash can. His words still ring in my ears. But now he's acting as if he never said a thing. So, does he want to be my friend or doesn't he?

I stop pacing. Ben's words about not trusting

Rudy filter through my mind. A nearby pillow tempts me and I kick it. The pillow flies through the air along with my Bible. It lands open with a thud.

"So?" Rudy says.

My chest feels tight and I don't know what to do. I feel like a cartoon character with an angel on one shoulder and a little demon on the other.

I can hear Rudy's breathing through the phone. My mind flashes from the bathroom scene to Rudy's words just now, "Had a blast last time."

When Rudy starts to speak again. I interrupt him. "Okay!" I blubber.

"Great!" Rudy blurts out. "I'll see you in an hour." He hangs up without allowing me to say another word.

The dull beep of the empty phone line numbs me for a minute. But then I'm back to pacing. Maybe I made the wrong decision. But I don't know. Maybe he didn't mean what he said in the bathroom. But I don't know. Maybe he really is a nice guy.

But I Just don't know!

I second-guess myself like this for the next hour while treating my floor like a treadmill.

By the time Rudy gets to my house, my heart is a storm of thunder. I let him in and we sit at the dining room table while Mom and Dad watch TV.

Mom had made brownies earlier in the day and she offers them to Rudy. "Have as many as you like."

Rudy bites into his first one. "These are awesome, Mrs. King." Then he fills his mouth with a second. "Thans fo makin 'em," he says through the chocolate, as nice as can be.

I sit next to him with my leg doing overtime work and my mouth empty. Brownies are the last thing I want to think about. Questions about Rudy's true plans occupy my brain.

He smiles at me with brown teeth and gives me a thumbs up.

I clench my fists. I can't sit here and act all nicey-nice when I still don't know why he said those things about me.

When I can't handle it any longer and he's moved on to brownie number three, I push my books aside. I can't wait any longer. It's time to get some answers.

I open my mouth to ask Rudy about his bathroom talk but nothing comes out. He stares at me with wide eyes and then gives me a questioning look. I swallow the lump growing in my throat and try again.

This time, instead of questions about the bathroom, I say, "Good brownies, huh?"

I don't even know where that came from. My mouth and my brain have become uncontrollable.

Rudy smiles and grabs brownie number four. "Yeah, your mom sure knows how to cook."

I nod my head in agreement and take a big bite of the last brownie.

If you can't beat 'em, join 'em. Right?

I take a peek at Mom and notice a faint smile. We must look like squirrels with mouths filled with our winter stock. I choke down the first big bite and then nibble on the rest while watching Rudy.

He's content as can be with crumbs covering his lips and a pencil in his hand. He looks a bit like an innocent 3-year-old getting ready to draw a picture for Mother's Day. A totally different image than what I had in mind earlier.

He wipes his sleeve across his face, licks his lips and grabs a piece of paper. "Ready?"

After my lousy excuse for a confrontation, I'm not sure I can try again, despite the fact that I still don't know anything about the Bathroom Incident.

Instead of making another attempt, I pull out my history book and move on to our most recent lesson. Rudy doesn't even seem to notice my failure. He listens as I talk about World War II and takes notes like a super-student. We spend the next two hours studying the war and then he goes home.

Since I failed at getting Rudy to talk, I have no answers. No explanations. And no way of knowing what's in his mind. Frustrated and confused, I skip dinner and go to bed early. I grab Wally and lie in my bed replaying our time in my head. I think of all the possible chances I had to say something. All of the missed opportunities to just blurt out the question, "Why did you say that?"

But I didn't do it and I still have questions. As I drift off to sleep, I promise myself that somehow I'll get to the truth.

At school the next day, I try to get Rudy's attention before class. I walk in and he's looking right at the door so I smile and wave to him. He smiles too and walks in my direction.

As he gets close, I hold up my hand to give him a high five. He raises his hand, too. "What's up, man?"

"Nothing much," I say and lean in to smack his palm.

But he walks right past me and leaves my hand hanging in the air. A jolt of uncertainty runs through my veins and I turn to see him high-five and fist-pump Max.

"Nada," says Max, "What's up with you?"
"Just ready for the weekend already," says Rudy.

"Ain't that the truth," says Max as he almost runs into me on his way past.

Neither one acknowledges my existence.

I take a quick check of the room to see if anyone noticed what just happened. Most kids are talking or pulling their books out of their backpacks. The warm comfort of relief fills me. That is, until, I turn to see Ben standing at the door with his lips twisted in disgust.

"I told you so," he says and pats me on the back. It's not the angry, ha-ha kind of "I told you so." It's more of the "I feel sorry for you" kind.

Ben shrugs and moves past me to his desk. For a moment, I'm frozen in place. I thought I knew where I stood with Rudy. But, once again, I have no idea. There's the nice Rudy and the not-so-nice Rudy and I'm not sure

which one is real.

Chapter 21
Ruined Redemption

The mystery of Rudy leaves me wound up tight for the rest of the week. By the time the weekend comes, he hasn't said a word or even looked me in the eye one time.

At least Ben is on my side again. If not, I might just sit in my room drooling and staring off into space–wondering if I'll ever have a friend again. But knowing that he has my back solves one of my problems.

I call him Friday night to remind him about the Saturday morning plan to take the recyclables to the drop-off, hoping he's still up for it. Relieved that he agrees, I try to get some shut-eye. But falling asleep and staying asleep seem impossible. I'm just too on edge, wondering how much money I'll collect.

I wake up way too early on Saturday with my mind still filled with thoughts of cans, bottles and dollar bills. Between the recycling and the yard sale money, I'd likely have enough to pay for a month's worth of groceries. After my trip to the redemption center, it would be time to combine it all and present it to my parents.

With that thought, I hop out of bed with a smile. Another one of my problems would be on its way to being solved today.

I pull on my jeans and a *Transformers* T-shirt and walk to the kitchen. The TV and the remote keep me company as I pass the time.

Alex wakes up around 7:30. He stumbles into the living room rubbing his eyes with one hand and holding his harmonica with the other.

"You want to come with us this morning?" I ask him.

He scratches his head, then his back, then his leg, never letting go of that harmonica. "What?"

"Ben and I are going to turn in the recyclables I have hidden at the back of the house." I open the curtains of the sliding glass door and point in the direction where I stashed the bags.

"Oh. I wondered what all that stuff was." He lies on the floor and stretches out. "Well, I'm not going with you. I need to watch my shows."

I sit back on the couch. "Whatever." I feel the remote under me and fish it out. "You'll see. By the time I'm done today, I'll have enough money to buy food for a month."

Alex ignores me and keeps his eyes on the television. I watch until I catch sight of the time, 8:00.

Time to get my money!

I drop the remote on Alex's lap, leave a note for Mom and Dad, collect the bags and take them to the garage.

When I open the garage door, Ben's already waiting on his bike.

"Told you I'd be here," he says.

"Thanks, man." I hook as many bags as possible to his bike and then do the same with mine.

My collection has grown so big that the handlebars of our bikes look like

elephant ears.

The bikes themselves are probably just as heavy. After the wobbly results of my crash at Balboa Park, the added weight makes me feel like I'm riding on a tightrope wire, ready to tip at any moment.

We take the ride slowly, side by side down the hill until we get to the redemption center. My mouth falls open when I see the line of people that hooks itself around the dirty old shack. Some of the customers look like they cleaned out every park in the city.

A few street people are also waiting with small bags in their hands. I look at Ben. Clenching his jaw, he stares at his watch then folds his arms across his chest without saying a word.

No telling how long we'd have to wait. I lift my hands, shrug and motion for him to follow me to the back of the line.

Despite the long wait, I get Ben to laugh by making up stories about the customers in line behind us. We imagine that the bald guy with about 50 bags of recycling is an aluminum can eating monster who wants to turn in his leftovers for cash.

After thirty minutes and another few good stories, we reach the front and I dump our load into five large tubs. I can't help but shake with excitement as I wait for the grand total.

The redemption man takes his time with our stuff though. He looks me up and down then runs his fat, gloved hands through each and every tub to make sure I haven't mixed the cans with the bottles.

When he's satisfied with my sorting skills, he weighs each tub, one at a time. Then he fills out some kind of form and has me sign it. Finally, he hands me a receipt.

No cash. Just a piece of paper.

"What's this? Where's the money?" I ask him, holding the paper out.

"That's your receipt," Redemption Man says, his large arms across his chest.

I fumble with the paper. "I know that!" Then I

crumple it and throw it in a trash can. "But where's my money?"

Redemption Man rubs his bald head and laughs. "Well, that's it right there." He points to the paper in the trash. "Take it inside the grocery store and they'll give you what it's worth." He shrugs. "That is …

… if you want it."

I drop to my knees and snatch the receipt from the trash. "Why didn't you say so?" I smooth it out on my jeans and look at Ben. He smirks, probably laughing inside.

I jump up and grab my bike. "Let's go."

Ben trails behind me saying something I can't make out. It sounds something like, "Here we go again."

I ignore him and take off toward the store across the street.

We leave our bikes locked to a skinny tree and go inside. While we stand in the checkout line, I review the receipt for my earnings.

A bunch of numbers and letters cover the paper from the top down. The bottom line says 30.00. But that couldn't possibly be the total. I figure it must be some kind of code and show it to Ben.

"What do you think that means?" I point at the 30.00.

"That's gotta be how much you earned." He nods his head. "Not bad."

"Not bad? Are you kidding me?" I shake the sheet

at him. "There's no way that's all I'm getting after all that work."

We reach the cashier and I hand it to her. She enters some numbers into her machine.

I watch and pray.

"Okay. Thirty dollars. Nice work. It's not often that a couple of kids bring in that much recycling." I wince at her squeaky voice as she counts the money into my hand.

Three ten dollar bills. That's it? Hours of time at the park, a bike accident, and a piece of glass in Ben's hand and that's all I earned? $100 would have been more like it. I would have even been happy with $75. But $30 feels like an insult.

I stuff the money in my pocket and leave the store in a hurry.

Ben catches up with me and grabs my arm. "What's wrong?"

"Just forget it. I have to get home. I'll see you later." I jump on my bike and take off without looking back.

When I walk in the front door, Mom, Dad and Alex are sitting at the kitchen table having breakfast.

"Already home from Ben's?" Mom asks.

"Yeah." For a second, I consider telling them everything I've done. But fear of their disappointment—and my own—stops me and I go to my room. "Uh, he's got stuff to do today," I say over my shoulder.

"You want some pancakes?" Mom calls to me.

"Uh, maybe later." I close my door behind me and sit on the floor. I pull the $30 out of my pocket and drop it in front of me. Alexander Hamilton's face mocks me from each $10 bill.

I leave them on the floor and grab the rest of the money from my sock drawer. I count it again just to be sure. It's still only $152. With the $30 I earned today it doesn't even make $200. I don't even know if it will be enough for groceries.

A knock comes at my door just as I'm putting the $182 back in my dresser.

"Yeah." I close the drawer and lean against it just as my mom opens the door.

"Why don't you come out and join us for breakfast." She moves her eyes around my room. "And then maybe afterward you can clean up in here."

I follow her eyes and take in the scene. In my opinion, it isn't too messy. Just some clothes, toys and books on the floor. At least all my coins are in neat piles on my dresser.

"I'm coming. I'll be there in just a sec."

Mom nods and closes the door. I open my dresser drawer one last time. The money is stuck between the edge of the drawer and the rail. I wiggle the drawer and try to slip one of the $20s from where it's wedged.

Only half comes out.

"Argh! No!" I put my hands to my head and let out a silent scream.

When I finish my noiseless fit, I give the other part of the bill a gentler tug. I fit the two pieces together and grab a piece of Scotch tape off my desk.

With the two pieces back as one, I give the bill a little kiss, fold it with the rest of the money and stick it inside a sock to keep it safe.

Remembering that pancakes await me, I walk to the kitchen. With the entire family eating breakfast together, it feels like old times. The only difference is that no one talks.

Mom sips her coffee but has a frown on her face and a far off look in her eyes. Dad keeps his head down looking at the computer screen, searching for jobs. And Alex has his eyes hooked to the TV.

No smiles. No chit-chat or, "How was school this week?"

I take a few more bites and feel a lump growing in my throat. I try to make it disappear with a swig of milk but it just gets bigger. Along with it, I can't stop shaking my leg.

Dad looks up at me when the table starts to move. I give him a smile, stuff another pancake bite in my mouth and catch Mom looking at me.

"Are they good?" she asks.

I nod. "Yeah." I think about the money in my sock drawer. "Uh, so how much do you guys spend on food every month?" I spit out the words as if they are choking me.

Mom is about to take a sip of her coffee but stops with it at her lips. She raises an eyebrow and sets the cup down. "Why do you ask?"

I look at the floor. "Just curious. Because, um ..." I search my brain for a good excuse. "... these pancakes are so good it much cost a fortune to make them."

Lame.

It takes a minute for Mom to answer. She picks up her cup again and spins it in her hands. "Well, we usually spend about $500 every month. But I've been trying to get it down to $300 now that your Dad's not working."

She looks over at Dad and he lifts his head. He gives a little frown and then goes back to scrolling on the computer.

I stare at the $500 pancakes and put my fork down. With only $182 in my sock, what am I

going to do now?

Chapter 22
Quite a Confession

My pancakes and milk sit cold on the kitchen table while I burrow back under my covers with Wally. I couldn't eat another bite after Mom's revelation about the cost of groceries.

I squeeze Wally next to me and try to go back to sleep. But there's a knock at my door and then Alex barrels into my room and jumps right on top of me.

"My turn to watch a show," he says.

I pull my head out of the blankets and glare at his back. He picks up the remote and clicks on the TV. He sets the volume to level 100,000 and the cartoon music drills needles into my ears.

"No it's not," I yell over the music and grab the remote from him. I click the TV off and throw the remote on the floor.

Alex gives me a dirty look. "We had a deal," he says, reminding me that selling his Wii games had cost me my TV choices for the month. "What's your problem?"

"Just leave me alone. Okay?" I hide my head again.

Alex doesn't move. But with him there, Wally can't relax. He bounces all over the bed, landing on my head more than once. Alex even encourages him with some trampoline tricks of his own.

I try to ignore them both but it's impossible to

sleep with a 9-year-old and a wiener dog playing bounce-house on your bed.

There's a moment when I wish I had super strength so I could fling the covers back and make both go flying into the air. I picture the ultimate shock they'd experience and I can't help but laugh.

"What are you laughing about under there?" Alex says and pokes me in the side.

His finger sinks into my ribs and I rip the blankets off with a grunt. "Ugh. Alex!" I sit up and scowl at him. "Get out of here!" I yell.

His eyes widen and he lowers his head. "Sorry. Let's go Wally." With a frown, he tucks the dog under his arm and slinks toward the door.

Suddenly feeling like the worst brother in the world, I take a deep breath. "Hey, Alex."

He turns and looks at me with wet eyes.

"You can stay. I didn't mean anything by it."

The frown disappears right away and his eyes turn happy again. "Thanks. So, what's wrong?" He sits down next to me and lets Wally burrow under the covers.

I'm not sure what to tell him. Part of me wants him in on my plan. But the other part of me doesn't trust that he'll keep it to himself. Including him would be a huge risk.

Deciding that I'm tired of being the only one coming up with the plans, I risk it.

"You haven't told Mom and Dad about my yard sale, right?" I ask.

He arches his eyebrows and looks at me like I'm crazy. "No!" He shakes his head. "You asked me not to. And I promised."

"Okay. I just wasn't sure." I adjust myself on the bed so I can look right into his eyes. "I want to tell you something, but you have to promise …"

I spit on my hand and hold it out to him,

"Promise not to tell."

He stares down at my hand and crinkles up his nose. For a minute he just sits there but finally spits in his hand and we shake on it. It feels a bit slimy but it gives me enough confidence to confess everything.

"Okay. My plan is to make enough money to buy the family groceries for a month. Mom says we need $300." I get up and go to my dresser. I pull the wad of money from my sock and lay it on the bed. "So far I have $182."

Alex picks up the money and rolls it around in his hands. He even smells it and rubs it against his face. It's a scene I'm familiar with. I guess he's more like me than I thought.

"Mmm. I like the feel of $182," he says.

I fidget with my pillow. "I know. But we need more. It's not enough. And I've done everything I can think of."

Alex sets the money down and gets up. He looks around my room. He says,

"We can sell more of your stuff."

Before I can say anything, a big smile grows on his face and he runs out of the room. Hearing his footsteps, Wally shoots out from under my blankets and follows him.

I wait, wondering what he's up to. After five minutes he comes back with a pair of shoes and a plastic gun used for one of our Wii games.

"What's that for?" I ask.

"We can sell this stuff, too." He holds up the shoes. "These Nikes cost Mom $100. They're brand new." He sets the Nikes down and then holds up the Wii gun. "This could get us $20."

I rub my head and think about it. But it doesn't take me long to come to a decision. "Let's do it."

I grab a pen and the first piece of paper I can find. Pushing the mess of old homework and toys off my desk, I turn the paper sideways.

"Okay, here's the plan." I draw a clock with the current time on it. 9:55 a.m. "This is perfect. Mom and Dad have to be somewhere at noon today." I write down 12:00 p.m. and put a picture of my parents next to it. "I'm supposed to babysit you."

Alex looks over my shoulder. "I'm not a baby."

I'm about to disagree with him but all I can think about is making sure our plan works. I draw a picture of a phone on the sheet. Under it I put 12:15. "So right after Mom and Dad leave, we'll start making phone calls. We have to get as many people over here as possible."

I write 3:30 as the final hour. "By the time Mom and Dad get home, everyone has to be out, money in our hands and all the stuff gone." I write THE SALE at the top.

Alex nods and looks around my room. "What else are we going to sell?"

I start another list. "I think it's time

to sell my TV."

Alex gasps. "Are you sure that's okay?"

"This is serious. We have to pull out the big guns." I continue writing. "Your Nikes, my Nikes, the Wii gun." I turn around and study every inch of my room. "I'll even sell a few of my coins."

Alex sits quiet for a minute. He rubs his chin, thinking. "We can sell my harmonica," he says in a quiet voice.

My mouth drops open. "Really?"

He nods. "It's okay. I bet someone will like it."

Even though Alex can be pretty irritating, he's a good little brother. I pat him on the back and scribble "harmonica."

By the time we finish, we have about 15 new things for sale. Alex and I collect the stuff and make a pile next to my TV. The minute Mom and Dad leave, we take it all into the living room and make a display on the coffee table.

I set the TV in the middle, to make sure everyone sees it. Surrounding it we put a bunch of Wii games, some DVDs and even my cell phone after I reset it, erasing all my personal information. Alex finds more toys he doesn't want and sets them in a basket next to the table. I set two coin booklets in front of it all as the icing on the cake.

Once we have everything displayed, I grab the house phone and start making calls. I go through the entire list from my seventh grade class. Then I call kids from the church youth group. I ask everyone to call at least one other kid. By 1:00, Alex and I are ready, waiting next to the front door.

When the doorbell rings for the first time at 1:15, my heart jumps. I look at Alex. His lower lip trembles and his eyes dart back and forth. He looks like he's been caught red-handed. I feel sort of the same way.

Suddenly, I'm not sure if I'm ready to sell all our stuff without Mom and Dad's permission.

Then the doorbell rings again and I cringe. I say to Alex,

"Should we really go through with this?"

Chapter 23
Tutors & Tests

Despite doubting THE SALE idea, I'm feeling pretty good as we finish and say goodbye to the last customer.

"Two-hundred dollars!" I say and wave the cash in Alex's face. "I can't believe we made this much."

Alex shakes his head in disbelief and points at the clock. "It's 2:45. Mom and Dad will be home soon."

With only fifteen minutes to get the house back to normal, my heart skips a beat. I take stock of the toys that remain and there isn't much.

We pile it all into a box and shove it in my room. As I'm about to close my door, I take a quick glance around and can't help but feel a sense of uneasiness when I catch sight of the empty space where my TV used to sit.

I click the door shut and return to the living room to make sure everything is back in place. When Mom and Dad get home at 3:00 not a sign of what we had done exists …

except for little twinges of guilt

... each time I think about my TV, my phone and everything else we sold.

No one bought Alex's harmonica, so I figure he'll be happy but even he seems a little down. Yet, he doesn't say so. After he says hello to Mom and Dad, he just falls asleep in front of a *Batman* cartoon.

When dinner comes, Alex fiddles with his fish sticks and then leaves most of them on his plate. Mom asks if he feels okay and kisses his forehead to feel for a temperature. Neither of us says anything to each other about the money or THE SALE.

Mom and Dad aren't very talkative either. The squeak from my tilting chair becomes very loud in all that quiet. Mom scrunches her eyebrows and wags a finger at me just as my name flies out of Dad's mouth loud enough to shock me into stillness, "Jacob Samuel King!"

I force the chair to the ground and gobble down my fish.

When dinner is over, I try to catch Alex's eye to have him follow me to my room, but he won't look at me. Instead I grab Wally to keep me company while I add up our new total. It now weighs in at $382. More than enough to buy groceries.

But why doesn't that make me feel better?

By the time I go to bed, my stomach feels like a raisin, all tight and dried up. I fall asleep with pangs of guilt and thoughts about Rudy.

Even my dreams are filled with Rudy. But he doesn't look like himself with all his red hair. Instead he looks like a giant red furball. The furball plays chase with me in Balboa Park and I think it wants to be my friend. But then it opens its mouth. Inside that big head is a mouth the size of a watermelon with gigantic shark teeth. It follows me around the park trying to bite my head off.

Sunday morning I wake up with a scream and find Wally at the end of my bed with his tail between his legs. I try to convince him to come to me, but he won't.

"I'm sorry, Wally." I pull him to me and cuddle him trying to shake off the memories of my dream.

But they won't go away. The picture of the giant furball with shark teeth flashes like a strobe light in my mind.

When the image finally fades, I remember THE SALE. The thought of it makes my stomach ache and gives me a bitter taste in my mouth. I look at the spot where my TV used to sit and I cringe. I'm going to miss that thing.

I shake my head and try to push away all the images. I check my clock. 8:30. Time to get ready for church.

The thought of Mom's usual wake-up call makes me shoot out of bed. She needs to stay out of my room until I'm ready to tell her what we did. Until then, she can't see that my TV is missing.

Or that I no longer have a cell phone.

I tear off my PJs and sling on some jeans and a shirt. I crack open my door, peer out and find her with her hand up, about to knock. I slip out the door and close it behind me.

Mom steps back. "Good morning. You're up early." She has dark circles under her eyes.

"Uh, yeah." I block the door. "I'm starving. Can I have some breakfast?" I rub my tummy to show her how hungry I am.

Mom narrows her eyes at me and then looks behind me to the door. "What's that noise in there?"

I hadn't noticed Wally scratching at the door. I open it just a crack and he bursts out down the hall. I make a forced chuckle and yank the door closed.

Mom stands with her arms folded across her chest. "Are you okay? Both you and your brother are acting pretty strange."

"No, I'm good."

I offer her a fake smile and leave her in the hallway, hoping she won't find a reason to go into my room.

When I don't hear my door cracking open, I take a seat at the kitchen table with a bowl of cereal and a huge sense of relief. Just as I stuff my first bite in my mouth, the house phone rings.

"Hello," I say through my cereal.

"Hey, it's me." It's the voice of the furball.

"Uh, hey Rudy." My heart beats a little faster thinking about the shark teeth.

"Why didn't you answer your cell?" he asks.

Mom walks in so I don't say anything.

"Anyway," Rudy goes on, "I need your help."

I close my eyes and try to picture Rudy as a kid

with a body and a normal head. "Help? With what?"

"I need extra credit for history. Uh, could you help me come up with another topic for a short report?" he asks.

My mind flashes to the bathroom conversation I'd rather forget. And then to the last time I tutored Rudy. He hadn't acted mean when he was at my house but he also hadn't talked to me since that day.

"So? Maybe tonight?" Rudy says.

I must be full of plans, because another one flashes in my mind. This time it involves Rudy. "Sure. Come over around 6:00."

I hang up the phone and dig into my cereal. Tonight would be Rudy's real test. Once we finish studying I'll ask him if he wants to hang out after school one day. If he says yes, I'll consider him a real friend. If he doesn't, then I'll know for sure what to think about Mr. Furball.

When Ben finds out about my study time with Rudy, he has a fit. We're in the middle of youth group on Sunday morning and his whisper becomes more like a bark, "What?" His lips twist into a frown. "You've got to be kidding me! You're going to hang out with him again? On a Sunday night? During our hang-out time?"

"You've gotta hear my plan." I give him a quick rundown of what I want to do with Rudy. Ben's eyes look blank. He's not impressed.

"If I were you, I'd just avoid Rudy altogether.

He's bad news." He says it loud enough to make the youth pastor stop preaching. He gives us a stern warning look and then keeps talking.

I keep quiet for the rest of the message. When group ends, I lean over to talk to Ben again but he gets up and walks out, without even a glance back.

I see him in the church service sitting several rows in front of my family. He never turns around but I watch his head until the service ends. As he walks by, I try to get his attention.

"Hey!"

He keeps on walking. His parents stop to talk with Mom and Dad for a minute, but Ben's out the door before I can say

"money."

My afternoon is spent lying on my bed, throwing a ball at the ceiling and trying to create a plan to work things out with Ben. But nothing comes to me. The only thing I can do is prove to him that he's wrong about Rudy. Or at least figure out the truth once and for all.

By the time Rudy rings the doorbell that evening, I'm feeling pretty crummy and need something to cheer me up. When Mom pulls out a box of microwave popcorn, I figure it will have to do.

I let Rudy in and he's all smiles, apparently in that "nicey-nice" mood again.

"What's up, Jake?" He nods to me on his way to the kitchen.

I bite my lip and stick the bag of popcorn in the microwave. I watch Rudy make himself at home at the kitchen table, pulling out his binder and pencils. Part of me wants to back out of my plan now that things seem normal again. But the other part of me is reminding me that

I might not be able to trust him.

I give myself an internal pep talk and pull the popcorn out. I fill a bowl, set it between us and we get to work. We don't talk much. It's all business. Rudy asks a few questions and I answer.

It's hard enough for me to sit with him without knowing the truth, but to offer help before I ask him The Question, is almost excruciating. At least the popcorn and the computer give me something to do with my shaky and fumbling hands. I pray that Rudy won't notice that my leg never stops moving.

After a very long two hours of chomping on Orville Redenbacher's and surfing the Internet, Rudy has a good start for a report on Pearl Harbor.

He looks over his notes while I grab a towel and start cleaning up our popcorn mess. He nods and smiles as he reads. "Thanks, man. You're a good friend." He closes his binder and sticks it in his backpack.

That comment stops me mid-swipe. I blink hard and turn to look at him. At first I can't find anything to say. When my voice finally comes back all I can squeak out is, "Sure." On top of that, my hands jitter so much I drop the towel.

When I lean to get it, I bump my head on the table and drop it again. Rubbing the growing knot on my skull, I bend and try again. But, trying to avoid injury to my head, I end up smashing my hand.

"You need some help?" Rudy asks.

I give up and sit on the floor massaging my hand and my head.

Rudy holds out his hand. "Come on. Let me help you."

I look at him, still in shock from his "friend" comment. I stare at his hand until he reaches down, grabs my arm and pulls me off the floor.

"You okay?" he asks. The way he looks at me, it seems like he actually cares.

"Uh, yeah."

"Okay. Well, I gotta go." Rudy picks up his notebook and heads for the door.

Then I remember my plan. I can't let him leave without going through with it.

"So, you want to hang out some day after school this week?" I ask, still feeling the pain of my bumps.

Rudy has his hand on the door handle. It takes a few seconds for him to turn around. When he does, he says, "Uh, I don't know if I have time this week." He pauses. "But that would be cool some other time."

I force myself to swallow. "Really?"

"Sure." He puts his hand back on the doorknob. "Uh, thanks for the help."

Then he leaves

without another word.

Chapter 24
Close to Collision

Neither Ben nor Rudy talk to me at school all week. I try to sit next to Ben in history class but he gets up and moves to another seat. I call him on Wednesday night to see if he's going to be at church but he won't come to the phone.

With Rudy, on the other hand, I don't try as hard. I see him in the hallway once and wave but he doesn't see me.

I guess.

It could be that he just ignored me. He and Ben could be twins with the way they're acting.

By the time Friday comes around, I don't even try to get their attention anymore.

On Friday night I hang out with Alex on the couch watching TV after Mom and Dad go to bed early. During the commercials I talk to him about giving them our money. He gets a sad look on his face when I bring it up.

"What's wrong?" I ask.

He looks at the ceiling. "I feel bad about what we did. I don't think they're going to be happy."

The muscles in my face tighten and I wobble my head to make it stop. "It'll be okay." Then the shaky-leg starts and I have to put my hand on it. "I think they'll understand."

Alex gives me a doubtful look. Then he shrugs

and turns his attention back to the TV. I don't feel like talking about it either, so I turn up the volume.

When TV gets boring, I go to my room. It isn't my fault that I hear Mom and Dad talking in loud voices again. This time I hear words like "house" and "move." To make sure, I get closer to their door.

Then Dad says, "I know. It might be time to sell."

No! It's my worst nightmare.

Moving was once just a possibility and now it could be real life! I run to my room, close the door and slide to the floor. The tears come and I bury my head in my hands to keep the noise from traveling to Mom and Dad's room. After a while, I feel myself drifting off to sleep.

I wake up the next morning on the floor. My back hurts and my legs sting when I stretch. Dried tears have left trails down my cheeks. When I yawn it feels like my face is cracking.

I pull myself off the floor and lie on my bed. The clock reads 9:00 a.m. For the first time in a month, I don't have a plan for the day. No new ways to make money. No way to help Mom and Dad.

The money in my sock doesn't even matter anymore. It isn't enough to save the house.

I feel the sting of tears again but I won't let them come this time. Instead, I drag myself off the bed and decide to get dressed. When I'm about to take off my pajamas I realize I'm not wearing them because I never changed my clothes. I look down at my wrinkled jeans and *SpongeBob* T-shirt and shrug.

I go to the kitchen to see who's awake and find it empty. Except for Wally, everyone else is still asleep. The silence feels too heavy but when Wally nips at my feet, I don't feel so alone.

I pace the kitchen with Wally at my heels until I can't stand the quiet any longer. I grab a granola bar and leave a note for Mom and Dad, thinking that a bike ride might help.

I pedal my wobbly bike to the park closest to my house and stop at the playground. The swings look inviting, so I climb on and pump my legs until I'm flying higher than the nearby trees.

When I grow tired, I drift until the swing slows and the glint of a penny catches my eye near the jungle gym.

I fling myself off the swing and grab the coin. A few feet away, I find another one. Once I have these, I walk the rest of the park looking for more. I find a few additional pennies and get back on my bike headed for other nearby parks to see what I can find.

At Park Number Two, I find 51 cents in pennies and nickels combined. By the time I get to Park Number Three, I'm feeling pretty hopeful. I leave my bike near the swing set and hunt for more coins. I don't find anything the first few minutes but then the sun glints off something big under the monkey bars.

As I move closer to it, I realize that it's a coin … a huge GOLD coin. I pick it up and turn it over in my hands. It looks like a silver dollar but it's not silver. It has the same president on the front, the same picture on the back and it's the same size.

But gold?

I rub it between my fingers, remembering the dream I had about a downpour of gold coins. My heart flips. This coin has to be something special, something worth more than the $2 Peculiar Penny I found. It could even be one of the amazing coins Grandpa always talks about.

I stuff the gold dollar in my pocket and start my ride toward home, feeling better than I have in the last two days. Images of money falling from the sky keep me tingling as I ride.

With my mind on Gold Coin, I don't notice a small rock on my way down a hill. I just hear it fling out from under my tire, so I look behind me to see where it went. My change in balance makes the bike wobble even more and I spin back around before I take another trip to the pavement.

Somehow, during the short time it took me to turn around, a bunch of kids showed up at the bottom of the hill and they're

blocking my path.

I try to steady my bike and smash my brakes. But I've picked up so much speed that I have to put my feet to the ground to slow myself. I skid, turn the wheel and end up sliding right next to the group.

Right away I realize that this isn't just any group of kids. It's Rudy and his friends.

By the time I stop in front of them, Rudy and all the guys with him have their eyes wide open.

I laugh with more than a few nerves showing. "That was awesome! Huh?"

No one says anything.

I look at Rudy. "What do you give it? A 10?"

Every head turns in Rudy's direction. The guys stare at him.

"Yeah, what do you think, Rudy?" asks Max. I hadn't notice before, but his voice sounds a little like Dora and Vader. I scowl at him.

Rudy looks back at Max and shifts back and forth on his feet. "Uh, I don't know." He glances around like he's searching for a place to hide. "I've gotta get home. I'm outta here."

Then Rudy takes off. He leaves the other guys just staring at the back of his red head.

"Well, I guess that must mean you got a zero

from judge Rudy," Max says. He walks up close to me and kicks one of my tires. "Zero's a good word to describe you anyway." He laughs real loud and the other guys join in.

My stomach knots and I glare at him but say nothing. I push my bike backward, ride around them and pedal as hard as I can to get away.

The ride up the next hill takes a lot longer than the ride down the last.

When I finally make it to the top, I look back and the group of guys is still in the same place and still laughing at me.

To my surprise,

Rudy is with them.

Chapter 25
Gold & Silver Surprises

fter seeing Rudy with the guys again, I ride like a wild man to get away from them. The wobbly tires don't even matter anymore. Escaping the park and those kids is my only goal.

I pump my legs and I feel the weight of the pennies in my pocket shift. They drift to the edge and almost fall out so I stop for a breather and make sure they slide back in. I look around to make sure the guys are no longer in sight and shake my head to rid myself of the confusing thoughts. But they won't go away.

Why did Rudy tell me, "You're a good friend," if he wasn't going to stick up for me? Instead, his eyes had been wider than Wally's when he's on his way to the vet.

I make sure all my coins are tight in my pocket and finish my ride home with my mind moving as fast as my tires. Just as I'm about to put my bike in the garage, I hear Mom in the backyard.

"So I can't have an opinion about this?" she yells.

I tiptoe to the fence and peek over.

Tears stream down Mom's cheeks as she moves close to Dad. "Look at me."

Dad starts pacing with his head down and arms tight against his chest. When I realize the state of things between them, I duck and glue myself to the fence. I find a small knot hole and peer in.

Dad doesn't look up. He moves back and forth without saying a word.

"So, that's it? You're not going to say anything else?" Mom's voice warbles.

Dad finally stops and raises his head. His face burns bright red. "Sharon. I'm the leader of this house." His voice booms. "If I say we need to sell the car, then that's what we're going to do."

After he speaks, Mom stares at him and cries even more. Then Dad walks back into the house.

I sink to the ground. I've never heard Mom and Dad fight like this before. It causes my mouth to go dry.

I watch Mom through the knot hole as she stands with her arms wrapped around her stomach and her body moving up and down with her sobs.

I can't be a witness to this and do nothing. I drop my bike in the garage and run into the house headed for the backyard.

As I'm about to open the back door, I hear Dad's voice.

"Jake, pack your things. You guys are going to Grandpa's for the rest of the weekend." His voice isn't as loud as it had been but it's tense enough to stop me in my tracks.

I turn with my hand on the door and force myself to swallow. "Can't we just stay home?"

Dad's eyes grow big and his lips turn into little lines.

I rip my hand from the door and walk toward my room. I spit out,

"Never mind. Just kidding."

"Grandpa will be here in an hour and a half. Be ready," Dad says as I reach my room. "Your brother is already packed."

"Okay." I lie on my bed and try to stop the heavy pounding of my heart. After a few minutes it returns to normal but my mind won't stop spinning. Why do we have to go to Grandpa's? Is it because of their fight?

I get up and throw a couple shirts and pants into my backpack then lie back down. I try to sleep while I wait but I can't. It's impossible to get any shut-eye with thoughts of Rudy, Ben and now Mom and Dad wrestling for space in my brain.

Trying to shut out the thoughts, I grab a Mason jar full of pennies and dump them on my bedside table. I pick through them one by one, studying them. I find one that's covered in dirt, so I use some spit and clean it with my shirt. When it comes clean I can't believe what I see.

It shows the face of Abe Lincoln but it doesn't look like a penny anymore. The dirt had given it a copper look but with a spit-clean shine the thing looks silver.

A silver penny?

I take the coin to the bathroom and run hot water over it. It's not until I almost burn my fingers that I pull it out. And, without a doubt, it's still silver.

The back of the penny looks the same as any other. I pull a coin from my pocket and compare them.

Same back. Same front. Different color. The date on Silver Penny reads 1943. I've never seen one like it.

I take all the coins out of my pocket and throw them in a pile on my bed. To it, I add the pile from my bedside table and as many pennies as I can find in my other coin boxes. I compare every penny to Silver Penny, looking for something to explain its existence.

After I've been at it for a while with no success, Dad knocks on my door.

"Grandpa will be here in five minutes. You ready?"

Distracted, I pick up another penny and mumble, "Yeah, just let me know when he gets here."

Dad cracks open the door. "Just be ready, that's all."

The creaking of the door gets my attention and I jerk my head up as I remember

my missing TV!

I jump off the bed and slide in front of the door. "Sure, Dad. I'll be out in just a minute. I just want to clean up some stuff." I block his way in.

"Clean up?" Dad snickers. "Okay. Clean up." His voice sounds like he doesn't believe me. But he closes the door anyway.

With a wipe of my brow, I go back to the coins. Just a little over half the pile remains. Feeling desperate to figure something out about the strange coin, I determine not to go to Grandpa's until I've looked through the rest of the stack. Maybe if I had another 1943 penny I could compare the two.

With so little time left, I swipe up a handful of the pennies and pile the ones with a different date on the bed. I'm just about to finish and I find it. 1943! Exactly what I was looking for.

But it's not silver.

I run to the bathroom and swish it in a sink full of soap and hot water. Nothing changes. I rub it a bit and it still looks copper. It's not quite as shiny as most of my pennies but it definitely isn't silver.

"Jake!" Dad's voice rings from the hall.

"Coming!" I sprint back to my room and snag my backpack. I stuff the two pennies into my pocket to show Grandpa.

The mystery of Silver Penny has my blood pumping. I pat my pocket to make sure the pennies are secure and feel something else in there. I grab at it and pull it out. It's Gold Dollar.

Perfect!

I slide the coin back in its place. Between the penny and the dollar, my pocket is now home to two coins that might just lift my mood and our family's finances for a while. Who knows what they could be worth, but they could change everything.

Maybe, just maybe, it will be a silver penny that pulls us out of this money predicament.

Grandpa attempts to make conversation on the car ride to Sacramento but I don't say much. Despite my excitement about the coins, Mom and Dad's fight is still on my mind and casts a shadow over everything.

I spend the hour and a half watching the rain beat against the giant windmills over the Altamont Pass. The day had started out nice and sunny but the weather had changed,

Just like my mood.

Once we arrive, Alex and I plop down on the couch in front of the TV. With the crummy weather, there isn't much else to do but watch cartoons. Grandpa brings us peanut butter and jelly sandwiches and settles down with us. We spend the evening that way, cuddled up in blankets and nibbling on snacks.

Once it's late, Alex and I turn out the lights in our room and I lie in bed thinking about the coins again. Despite trusting Alex with my latest "plans," I'd rather keep the coin stuff to myself until I know more about them. I wait until his heavy breathing assures me he's asleep and slip out of our room to find Grandpa. He's back in the living room sitting in his recliner with the TV on.

All the lights are off so I tiptoe up to him, just in case he's asleep.

"Grandpa," I whisper.

He jumps out of his chair and spins around with his fists up, like he's ready for a fight.

His eyes grow big when he sees me. "Jake! You nearly scared me to death." He holds his heart. "I thought you were sleeping."

I chuckle. "Sorry, Grandpa. I thought you were too."

He takes a few deep breaths then sits back down and flips on the lamp nearest him. "What's going on?"

"I want to show you something," I whisper. I place the gold dollar and the two pennies on top of a pile of books.

"Look at that." I point to the dollar. "Have you ever seen anything like it?"

Grandpa squints. "Hand me my reading glasses. They're on the coffee table."

Sweaty palms give away my nerves as I pass him the glasses and then rub my hands on my PJs.

Ignoring the moisture, Grandpa puts his glasses on and places the coin close to his face, studying it. "Hmmm."

The minute he says, "Hmmm," my fidgeting starts.

In what seems like slow motion, he turns the coin over in his hand a million times. With the dollar next to his eye, he finally says, "Get me my pocket knife from the kitchen drawer."

He doesn't give a reason or an explanation, but I run to the kitchen and fumble through the drawer until I find it.

I hand the knife to him with shaky fingers. "What are you going to do with it?"

"Watch." He opens it and uses the blade to scratch a line right down the middle of Eisenhower's face. He puts the coin under the lamp.

"Look at it real close."

I lean over and try to get a good look.

I can't believe what I see.

Chapter 26
Scratch and See

A fake. Nothing more than a fake?

I turn the coin over in my hand, just like Grandpa did. It's just a silver dollar spray painted gold!

Why didn't I see it?

"Sorry, Jake." Grandpa closes up his knife and hands the coin back to me.

"I should have known." I shove the dollar in my pocket without looking at it again and plop down on the couch. "I can't believe I couldn't tell. Shows you what kind of coin collector I am."

Grandpa wrinkles his eyebrows and clears his throat. "Do you want to know how to tell the difference?"

I look at the ground. "I've been collecting coins for a long time, Grandpa. I should already know."

He sits and squeezes my shoulder. "There's only one real way to recognize a fake." He pauses and gets close to my ear. "You have to know what the real thing looks like," he whispers.

"Huh?"

"The real thing." A smile grows on his face and he lifts his eyebrows like I should know what he means.

I shrug and just look at him. We stare at each other for a long time until he gets up and goes to the back of the house. When he returns he's holding a silver dollar in his hand.

"Look at this." He opens my hand and sets the coin in it. "Tell me what you see."

"It's just a silver dollar."

And it feels cold.

"Tell me what a silver dollar looks like." Grandpa leans back on the couch.

I don't understand but I try to play along. "Okay. A silver dollar has President Eisenhower on the front. And the back has an eagle flying above the moon."

Grandpa smiles but keeps quiet. He nods his head

and gestures for me to keep talking.

The coin looks just like all the other Eisenhower silver dollars I've ever seen–nothing special about it.

They all look the same.

The minute that thought comes to mind, I understand Grandpa's point. "They're all silver!" I jump up from the couch. "That's it, right? There's no such thing as a gold Eisenhower dollar. They're all the same."

Grandpa's smile is even bigger now and he breaks into a hearty laugh. "You've got it." He gives me a high five. "And you already knew that. You just got a little excited about the gold."

The gold. Yep. I was pretty excited. "But, why would someone spray paint a coin?"

I pull it out of my pocket and sit back down. The scratch Grandpa made down the middle stares back at me. "Can I have your knife, Grandpa?"

He hands me the knife and I take to scratching off the rest of the paint like a dog chewing on a bone. I press so hard that I leave a permanent mark on the back of Eisenhower's head.

"Slow down there." Grandpa taps my arm. "You're going to end up cutting yourself."

"Why would a person want to trick someone like this?" I slow the scratching but don't stop. I turn it over and go to work on the eagle.

Grandpa shrugs. "I guess some people think it's

fun to fool others." He touches my hand again reminding me to slow down. "No one likes a fake, huh?"

With that statement, I stop. Rudy's face has just popped into my mind. I fiddle with the coin as I picture Rudy and Max the last time I saw them–staring at me as I rode my wobbly bike away from the sound of Max's mocking.

"That's for sure." My hand aches a little so I set the knife and the coin down. "That's kind of the way I feel about this kid at school. I don't know if he's a real friend or a phony."

Grandpa rubs his chin for a minute. "Well, how can you tell the difference?"

I stare at the ceiling and think about it. Grandpa takes my hand and sets his silver dollar in it.

"I guess it's kind of like a coin," I say, turning the dollar over. "I just need to know what the real thing looks like."

Ben comes to mind along with images of

the yard sale
AND
his cut hand
AND
the trip to the recycling center.

I let out a sad sigh.

Grandpa leans and looks into my eyes. "You can always trust a real friend, Jake." He picks up his Bible from the small table next to his chair. "I call this the Real Thing because

You can always trust it too."

He holds it tight to his chest. "And with a phony, all you have to do is scratch the surface and his true colors will come through. Just like with your coin."

The tension I'd felt growing in my chest releases its grip. Grandpa had found the solution to my Rudy problem. I give him a big hug. "That's it, Grandpa!"

All I'd have to do is "scratch the surface" with Rudy. I grab Gold Dollar off the coffee table and give it a kiss. It will be my inspiration. The next time I see Rudy, it will be my chance to find out whether he's a fake or a real friend.

I give Grandpa another hug. "Thanks a lot, Grandpa. Goodnight." With the coin still in my hand, I walk back toward my room with a bounce in my step. Just as I'm about to open the door, I remember Silver Penny.

Both 1943 pennies were still on the coffee table. And I hadn't even asked Grandpa about them. I'd never be able to sleep if I didn't get more information about those two, so I make a U-turn.

"I forgot my pennies." I plop back down on the sofa and grab them off the table. "Look at these

Grandpa." I hold them under the light and Grandpa puts his glasses back on.

"You've got yourself a steel penny there. That's a nice find." He nods his head.

"It's steel? Not silver?" I frown.

"Yep. They made them for a while during World War II because they had to use all the copper for weapons." Grandpa clicks off the TV and looks closer at the coins in my hand. "Hmmm." He takes Copper Penny from me. "Now this is strange."

strange?

I thought that's what he'd say about the steel penny, not the copper one. I take a closer look. It's just like any other penny, except it isn't quite as shiny.

Grandpa says, "Hmmm," again and walks into the kitchen with the coin.

There's no way I can just sit and wait while he's making all those noises. Especially since he doesn't even tell me what "hmmm" means.

I follow him to the kitchen and find him searching through his junk drawer. He's no longer slow, his hands move like lightening.

"Uh, Grandpa? What are you doing?"

All I get back is a finger waving in the air letting me know that I need to wait.

"Ah-hah. Here's one." Grandpa knocks some stuff out of the drawer and onto the floor. He doesn't even pick it up. When he turns around he holds up a magnet. "Are you ready?"

I scratch my head. "Ready for what, Grandpa?"

He laughs. "Oh, sorry. I got too excited." He sits down at the kitchen table and motions for me to do the same. "This here penny could be just the 'something special' you've been looking for." Grandpa's mouth is moving as fast as his hands. He takes a breath before he continues. "Remember what I said about the steel pennies?"

"Yeah."

"They didn't make many copper pennies in 1943." He holds my penny up for me to look at. "If they did, it was a mistake. So there are just a few out there. And they're worth a lot of money because they're so rare."

Worth a lot? That makes me sit up straighter.

"Maybe even thousands of dollars." Grandpa moves the magnet and the penny a few inches away from each other. "But ..." he looks at me again. "... some people liked to paint the steel pennies to make them look copper. Just the way they did with your gold dollar."

That brings a frown to my face.

Another painted coin? That's all I need. Another fake.

"But, I already scratched this one a little bit and it doesn't seem to be painted." He scoots his chair a little closer to mine. "Now all we have to do is the real test."

I try to keep my hands from twitching and swallow to steady my voice. "Well, let's do it."

"A magnet will stick to any steel penny. But if it's copper, it won't." He holds the magnet in one hand and the penny in the other.

Chapter 27
Penny Problems

randpa inches the magnet and the coin closer and closer together. I force myself to breathe and grip the edge of the table.

Then they touch. And nothing happens. They don't stick. Grandpa moves the penny all over the magnet and it just slips off.

I swallow the lump in my throat. "Does that mean it's real? Am I going to get thousands of dollars?"

Grandpa shakes his head and smiles.

"No? It's not real?" I grab his arm and rattle him a bit. "Grandpa, say something. I can't read your mind!"

My shaking makes Grandpa drop both the coin and the magnet on the table with a clink. He pushes his chair back and takes the magnet back to the drawer without a word. He picks up the stuff he dropped on the floor and then comes back to me. He sets a hand on my shoulder.

"Listen, Jake. Let's not get too excited."

I cover my eyes with the palms of my hands. "Grandpa!"

"Okay." He pauses. "Yes, it might be real."

I jump out of my chair like a rocket. "Yes! Yes!" Nothing can keep me down when I hear that. I dance around the kitchen, pumping my fist in the air.

"But we have to get an expert opinion before we know for sure," he says.

I stop jumping. "Okay. When? How? Just tell me what to do and I'll do it."

Just then Alex walks into the kitchen rubbing his eyes. "What's going on? Why are you making so much noise?"

Grandpa looks at his watch. "It's 11:30, Jake. You need to get to bed." He turns to Alex. "Sorry for waking you."

Grandpa puts his arms around both of us and leads us to our room. "Go to sleep. We'll take your penny to a coin shop in the morning."

He has to be crazy if he thinks I can sleep after news like that. I give him a hug and turn out the lights but lie in bed on top of the scratchy quilt staring at the ceiling. The nightlight creates funny shadows and I add to them by making images with my fingers. I picture different animals battling against each other as I watch the hours tick by on the clock. I end up staying awake all night and when the time finally reads 6:00 a.m., I shoot out of bed.

I get dressed and try to make as much noise as possible to wake up Alex. He doesn't move a muscle. I even lean down and say his name a few times into his ear. I get a little grunt out of him but nothing more.

At 6:07 I give up and go to the kitchen to pour myself a bowl of cereal. The penny still lies on the table where we left it. I pick it up and look at both sides again. Hard to believe that something so small could be worth so much money.

It's 6:17 when I finish my cereal and Grandpa and Alex are still asleep. I turn on the TV and try to keep my mind busy by watching cartoons. But every show I find reminds me of the money.

On one show a rabbit finds a treasure chest full of gold. On another a mouse earns a reward for finding a bad guy. There had to be something that would keep me from thinking about money!

Grandpa's Bible, his Real Thing, catches my eye. It sits where he left it on the couch last night. I look at it, at the TV and then back at the Bible.

I hit the remote and turn off the TV. The Bible has a bookmark in it, so I pick it up and open it to that spot. It opens to exactly the same verse Grandpa read to me the last time we were at his house.

I read it aloud.

If only things were that simple!

I trace the words with a finger. Maybe this coin is God's way of making sure I don't have to worry. A coin worth thousands of dollars could save our house and our car for sure.

I lean my head back and stare up at the ceiling as I think about the possibilities. The next thing I know, Alex is shaking me, telling me to wake up. I open my eyes and they feel heavy. I'm still on the couch, but a blanket covers me and a pillow lies under my head. I look around. Grandpa sits in his chair watching TV just like last night.

"What time is it?" I ask.

"12:00. You've been asleep all morning," Alex says.

12:00! I throw the blanket aside and jump up. "We've gotta go. Grandpa, let's go." I go straight for the front door.

"Whoa. Wait a second." Grandpa gets up. "Let's talk about our plan for the day and then we can get going."

"You slept through church," Alex says.

"We didn't even go because of you."

I look at Grandpa to see if it's true. He nods. "I figured you needed your sleep."

"Sorry."

"Besides, it looked like you had a little church of your own before you went to sleep." He points to the

217

Bible that still lies open to the page I read.

The verse rings in my head. *Don't worry.* I still put my hand on the doorknob. "Can we go get my coin checked out? Please."

Grandpa looks at Alex. "You ready?"

"I guess so," Alex says.

It takes twenty minutes to get to the coin shop. My palms sweat the entire way. And my stomach hurts so much, I think I might throw up. When we pull into the parking lot, I figure Grandpa has made a mistake. The little store is in a shopping center that looks older than the coin itself. A dead tree stands near the front of the building with trash littered around its trunk.

We have to be buzzed in through a door covered with bars. Once inside, it clangs shut behind us. It reminds me of my fifth grade field trip to Alcatraz when they closed us inside a prison cell and slammed the door.

The thought of it rattles me and I try to shrug it off.

I keep close to Grandpa and Alex but take a look around. The place

Smells like cats.

I immediately find out why. When we walk up to the counter a fluffy white cat crawls out from under and wraps its tail around my leg. I try to shoo it away but it keeps coming back. I nudge Alex and point to it. He just laughs.

The owner of the shop is on the phone. He rubs a scruffy beard and waves with an unlit cigar in his hand. Between the owner, the trash outside, the bars, and the cat I don't feel good about this place. "Maybe we should go," I tell Grandpa.

He tilts his head to the side. "What? We finally made it here and now you want to leave?"

"This place gives me the creeps."

Grandpa chuckles. "This is the best coin guy I know when it comes to rare items."

Coin Guy hangs up the phone and comes to the counter. "How can I help you?" He's tall and super thin. And really old. Probably older than Grandpa if you go by the number of wrinkles on his face.

Grandpa pulls out my penny. "We think we have a rare coin here. We're wondering if you could appraise it for us."

Appraise? I tug on Grandpa's sleeve. "What does that mean? I just want to find out how much it's worth."

"Jake," Grandpa shakes his head. "That's what 'appraise' means."

Coin Guy takes the penny and sets it on a piece of cloth under a huge magnifying glass. He flips a switch and a bright light comes on, shining through the glass. He leans close to the coin and looks at both sides. Then he scratches it with the nail on his pinky finger, which happens to be his only long fingernail. Like I said, creepy.

"Hmmm," Coin Guy says.

Why does everyone always have to say "hmmm"? A few words would help.

"What do you think?" Grandpa asks.

"This one looks promising. Could be worth something." He clicks off his light and pushes the magnifying glass out of the way. "But I'd have to send it to my guy in L.A. **to be sure.**"

Chapter 28
Faking Friendship

Coin Guy tells Grandpa it will take one or two weeks to find out anything more about my coin. They stuff it in a tiny padded envelope and ship it off to Los Angeles.

During the entire week afterward I can't sleep at night. Whether it's the coin or wondering how to deal with Rudy, my body won't cooperate to get any shut-eye.

By the beginning of the second week, I can barely keep my eyes open at school. On Tuesday, Mr. Birgdon taps me on the shoulder to get my attention in history class. I stuff my fists into my eyes to get the sleep out and pencil in an answer to a history question written on the board.

When class finishes, out of the corner of my eye, I see Mr. Birgdon moving my way. Before he gets to me, I grab my things and slip out of the room, heading to the bathroom to splash water on my face.

Despite feeling relieved to have escaped Mr. Birgdon's likely questions about my sleepiness, I'm still rubbing my eyes when I enter the bathroom. I hear familiar voices and feel a strange twinge of uncertainty. Lowering my hands, I see that it's Rudy, Max and three of their friends, all hanging out around the sinks. Rudy hasn't talked to me since our last extra-credit tutoring session and I'm not sure what to do. I turn and start to walk out.

But then I change my mind.

Instead, I walk right up to Rudy and hold up my hand for a high five.

It's time to set things straight. Time to find out what kind of guy Rudy really is. I'm tired of guessing, tired of not knowing if I can trust him.

"Hey, man. What's up?" I wait with my hand in the air but he just looks at me until I put it down. "When are you going to come over again? Maybe we can hang out and watch a movie this weekend." I look at the other guys as they watch Rudy.

Rudy's eyes widen. He twists his head around, eyeing the exit.

"So you gonna hang out with this nerd?" Max says, glaring at me.

Rudy smirks and shakes his head. "Are you kidding me?" He laughs and smacks Max on the shoulder. "My grade in History is awesome. What do I need him for now?"

My heart sinks.

And the guys keep laughing. Suddenly it sounds like I've gone underwater. And everything seems far away. Like I'm not even there anymore, which sure would be nice. To escape. To go hide in a cave somewhere.

Then it gets worse.

Max, at least a foot taller than me, moves so close that I can feel his hot breath in my hair. He takes hold of my hoodie and pulls it over my face.

"What should we do with him now that you're

done with him?" Max's Dora-Vader voice booms.

I want to run out but my feet won't let me. I'm stuck to the bathroom tile. I yank the hood back and try to stand taller than usual. Maybe that would make Max back off.

But it doesn't work. He sucks in his chest and stands even taller than before. Then he pushes me against the sinks. The counter edge digs into my back and I wince. I don't want to show fear, to let them know that I'm about to pee my pants, but I can't help it. I just close my eyes, pray for help and prepare for the pounding.

When it doesn't come right away, I don't open my eyes. I just clench my muscles and wait … until I hear the door creak and the sound of someone drawing in a shocked breath.

"What are you guys doing?"

I pop my eyes open and see Ben standing at the entrance to the bathroom. My head spins from him to Max and back again. Ben's eyes flame and he has his fists clenched, looking scarier than I've ever seen him.

It's a good thing he's on my side.

Max still has me up against the sinks but when he sees Ben he steps back. Rudy and the other guys move even farther away.

"You need some help, Jake?" Ben stomps over to me, his face red as he places himself between me and the other guys.

Max ignores Ben and scowls at me.

"Uh, yeah." My answer comes out as a squeak.

Ben folds his arms across his chest and plants his feet. "Get lost you guys."

Rudy pulls on Max's shirt. "Let's get out of here. It's not worth it."

Max whips his head around and looks at the group of guys. They all gawk at him with wide eyes. One of the shorter boys motions toward the door. Max turns back to Ben, who hasn't moved.

Letting out a laugh that echoes through the stalls, Max fidgets with his notebook. "Yeah, sure. These two aren't worth much anyway."

Once Max seems to have given them permission to go, all four boys sprint for the door.

Rudy doesn't even look back.

Alone, without backup, Max seems shorter. "Whatever," he says. His voice sounds more like Dora than Vader now. He slinks out of the bathroom.

The minute he leaves, I double over, holding my stomach.

"You okay?" Ben asks.

I draw in a few deep breaths and stand up. "Yeah, just checking the floor for coins," I joke. I try to offer him a fake smile but my mouth is stuck open in shock.

Ben shakes his head and pats me on the back. "Always the joker, huh?" He motions toward the door. "How did you get into it with those guys anyway?"

It was my fault. I knew it. I asked for it. I wanted to "scratch the surface" with Rudy to see if he was a true friend.

I guess it worked. I found out what I wanted to know.

I lean back against the closest sink. "You were right." I barely choke it out.

Ben puts his hand to his ear. "What?"

"You were right," I yell, the sound bouncing off the bathroom walls.

Ben smiles, putting his other hand up to his opposite ear. "Eh? I can't hear you. I think you said that I was right?" He leans closer to me, acting like he's trying to hear me better.

"If you want me to beg forgiveness, I can." I get down on my knees and fold my hands. "Please, oh, please! Can you ever **forgive me?"**

Chapter 29
Time to Talk

Ben grabs my hands and pulls me to my feet. "I guess that's good enough. Get up." He checks the door to make sure the guys are gone. "You are my best friend after all."

The pumping of my heart starts to slow and I place a hand on my chest. "Let's get out of here."

Together we check outside for the guys and there's no one in sight. "Come on, I'll walk you home," says Ben.

I bristle a little at his offer. "I'm not a little kid. I can walk by myself."

The look on Ben's face reminds me of the lesson I learned just seconds ago. I need to trust him. To know that he means well and wants to help. I need to remember that he's a

true friend.

"Sure, walk home with me," I say with a confident nod.

On the way, we joke about the possibility of my face being plastered to the bathroom walls.

"I would have come by and graffitied my name on your nose." Ben laughs as we pass by the cotton candy colored house near the elementary school.

"Very funny," I say. "Maybe by the end of the

school year I would have become a valuable piece of art."

When we get to my house, Ben looks me up and down. He scratches his head and shifts on his feet. "Well, I'm glad you're alive." He holds his fist out.

I fist-pump him and stare at him for a moment. Grandpa was right. The only way to tell the difference between the real thing and a fake is to know what the real thing looks like.

And Ben iS it!

"Catch ya later. I don't think those guys will be bothering you anymore," he says and walks in the direction of his house.

After Ben leaves, I stay on the sidewalk in front of my house for a moment. Knowing that Rudy has been faking friendship all this time has left me both disappointed and disgusted. Mostly disgusted with myself for letting him trick me and for not trusting Ben.

Hoping that I've learned my lesson, I go inside, ready to spend the evening in front of the TV. A little bit of time to relax and think about nothing would be nice.

I walk down the hall to my room, pulling off my hoodie as I go. Just as I'm about to turn the nob to my bedroom door, I remember that I no longer own a television. I sold it at The Sale.

Again, I'm disgusted with myself.

Planning to watch in the living room instead, I

open my door to leave my backpack and hoodie but find Mom and Dad both sitting on my bed.

Dad motions for me to come in. "Jake, we need to talk to you."

I eye my empty TV area. There's no way they didn't notice. Bracing myself for what's to come, I try to keep my voice calm. "Uh, what's going on?"

A piece of paper is in Dad's hand. He gets up and holds it out to me. "I've made a list of the things that are missing." His eyes shift to Mom and then back to me. "Your TV, your new Nikes, your phone, your–"

"You can stop." I hold out a hand to interrupt him. "You don't have to read any more. I know what's missing."

Mom gasps and gets up. "What have you done?"

I go to my dresser, pull out The Sock and hand it to Dad.

"A sock? What's going on, Jake?" Dad holds it in his open palm. "This isn't time for messing around."

"Look inside," I say and sit down.

Dad fiddles with it for a minute and then pulls out the bills. "What's this?"

Mom gasps again.

He sets down his list and counts the money. When he finishes, he looks at Mom. "$382." He drops the money as if it were on fire. "Where did that come from?"

Hoping they'll forget about HOW I got the money when I explain everything, I begin to get excited.

I start with the good part.

"It's for you," I say.

They look at each other, their eyes filled with confusion.

"Where did you get it?" Dad repeats.

"Use it to buy groceries. Or pay the car payment. It's yours." I smile, feeling at least a little pleased with myself amidst the fear of their possible reaction.

Mom doesn't smile. Instead, she starts to cry. Dad puts his arm around her.

"Did you sell your things to earn money for us?" Dad asks. Mom holds onto him so tight I can see the veins in her hands.

"Yeah." I can't help but feel pride as I look at the almost $400. I'd worked hard for it. But there's quiet from both my parents and the silence doesn't give me much confidence.

After what seems like enough time to ride to Balboa Park and back, they sit back down on the bed, one on either side of me. Mom grabs my hand and holds it between hers.

"I'm so sorry," she sobs. "You're in big trouble … but I'm so sorry."

I'm not sure whether to feel sad or scared. My hand starts to jitter inside hers.

"This is our fault," she says. She squeezes my hand tighter. "Your fault … but ours."

My hand is starting to hurt.

Confusion is all I have to hold on to. "Uh, I know you probably didn't want me to sell my stuff. But aren't you happy?" I pull my hand away, grateful for a break, and grab the money. I hold it out to her but she doesn't take it. "This will help." I look back and forth between them and try to keep my shaky leg still. "We won't have to sell the car."

Dad clears his throat and pats Mom's back. "Well, this isn't what we expected." He looks me right in the eye. His fill with tears. "This wasn't the right thing to do, Jake." He clears his throat again and then swallows so loud it sounds like a bullfrog at midnight.

"But your mom is right. Part of this, just a part …" He emphasizes it, " … is our fault."

Dad stands. He takes the bills in his hand and stuffs them back in the sock. His hands are red as he rubs them across his head and paces the room.

While he paces, I try to massage away the pain from Mom's grip. Then she takes my hand again, so I draw in deep breaths and try not to focus on my fingers turning blue.

I count the number of times Dad moves from one side of the room to the other.

One, two, three … twenty five, twenty six …. thirty five …

Finally, he jerks his head up. "We haven't shown you how to trust God," he spits out.

His sudden revelation causes me to jump a little. "Huh?" I look at Mom. She sobs even harder. I twist my hand out of her grip and rub her back.

"It's okay. God showed me what to do."

Dad lets out a long and loud breath. "Thanks for trying to help."

His "thank you" doesn't sound serious.

Dad puts his hand on my shoulder. "But, God wants us to trust him. And I'm pretty sure that doesn't mean going behind your parents' backs and selling your stuff."

My Jaw tightens.

I stop rubbing Mom's back. It's my turn to pace as my parents watch. "But, I did it to help. Isn't that what God wants?" I kick my backpack out of my way.

Mom doesn't let me pace long. She takes my hand again and pulls me down onto the bed. "You help best when you're honest."

The weight of her words hits me. I'd been lying to them thinking it was the right thing to do. I even thought that God gave me the idea. I bow my head and stare at the floor. How could I have been so wrong?

"God will take care of us, Jake." Mom lifts my chin. "And we should have done a better job of showing you that we believe that."

My heart tells me she's right. "I'm sorry. I ... I was wrong."

For the second time in one day, I had to admit I'd made a big mistake. My eyes fill with tears and I wipe them away.

Alex pops his head in the door just as Mom is giving me a hug.

He looks at Dad then at Mom and cringes.

"Uh, Grandpa Lou's on the phone for Jake," he

says and then closes the door fast.

My skin turns numb with the thought that he may be calling about the penny. "Can I?" I ask.

Mom lets out a loud breath and looks at Dad. Dad's lips are tight for a minute but then he lets them go loose and nods. Mom pats me on the back. "Go ahead."

"But we'll talk more about this later," Dad calls after me as I sprint to the living room.

I pick up the phone and lift up a short prayer for forgiveness and for help before I speak.

"What's up Grandpa?"

"I'm coming to get you," he says. "I got a call

about your coin."

Chapter 30
Reading the Report

Coin Guy's shop smells just as bad as the last time but I don't hold my breath. I stand at his counter with his cat wrapped around my leg and my heart pounding half out of my chest. The old guy takes his time finding my coin in the back of the store.

When he finally brings it out, he lays it on the counter wrapped in a black velvet cloth. He opens it and my penny lies there with Abe Lincoln staring up at me. "So?" I can't hold it in any longer. "What did you find out?"

"One more second, son," Coin Guy says and disappears to the back of the store again.

I shift back and forth on my feet and look up at Grandpa.

"Patience," he says.

Coin Guy comes back with a sheet of paper in his hand. "This here's the appraiser's report. It describes your coin and tells how much it's worth." He holds it out. "Who wants to see it first?"

I snatch it from his hand. Lots of words cover the top of the page so I scan down to the bottom where I see the dollar signs. I have to blink hard to make sure my eyes aren't playing tricks on me. I count the zeroes and make sure the comma is in the right place.

"$8,500!" I choke out.

Coin Guy chuckles. "Don't that beat all?"

Grandpa puts on his reading glasses and takes the paper from me. He studies it for a minute. When he finishes reading, he looks up at me with his mouth open. "It's real."

By the time Grandpa gets me back home it's nearly 11:00. Mom and Dad are in bed, so we pound on their door to wake them up.

Mom comes out first. "Dad?" She studies Grandpa. "What's going on?"

"You have to see something," I say.

She raises her eyebrows and looks between me and Grandpa. Grandpa gives her a giant grin and motions for her to follow us to the living room.

As she pulls on her robe and follows us down the hall, Dad stumbles out of the room.

"What's going on? Jake? Lou?" Dad rubs his eyes.

"Sit down. I have something to show you," I announce.

Mom and Dad do as they are told, likely because Grandpa's there and not just me. I lay the velvet cloth with my penny on the coffee table in front of them. Neither says a word. They look at the coin, then at each other and then at me.

Dad clears his throat. "You woke us up to show us a penny?"

"Yep." I say and hand them the appraiser's report.

Dad scans it then makes the same face Grandpa did when he read it. Mouth open.

Mom starts crying.

It's not the loud sobbing kind of crying. Just quiet tears running down her cheeks.

"It's all yours," I say.

Dad grips Mom's hand and looks up at Grandpa Lou.

He just shrugs.

"You can use it to pay bills." I sit down next to them. "Or whatever you want."

Neither says anything. They look at each other for a minute and then Dad stands. He pats me on the back and picks up the coin. "This is great, Jake. I'm proud of you."

For some reason,

he doesn't sound as happy as I thought he'd be.

He pulls me to him and hugs me tight. "Mom and I need to talk about what we're going to do with the coin." His voice grows quiet. "Why don't you head to bed and we'll talk with you about it in the morning."

The uncertainty in his voice makes me look to Grandpa. "You heard your dad. Get some rest."

There isn't much else I can do but go to my room. As I'm about to walk inside, I take one last look back down the hall. Dad has his arm wrapped around Mom. She's no longer crying. She just whispers something to Grandpa and he nods.

The answers about their plans would have to come some other time. I change my clothes and fall into bed. Despite not knowing what Mom and Dad are going to do with the coin, I get the best night's sleep I've had in a long time.

I wake up at 10:00 the next morning and pull Wally to me. I lie in bed petting him for the next half hour. At 10:30 I hear a light knock.

"You awake?" Alex asks.

"Yeah, you can come in."

With that, Alex barrels into the room and jumps on the bed, almost smashing Wally.

"I heard about your coin," he says.

I jolt to a sitting position. "What did you hear?

What did they say?"

Alex grabs Wally and snuggles with him on the bed. "Just that you have a cool coin and it's worth money."

I Jump Out Of bed.

I leave the two of them in my room and go to the kitchen where I find Mom, Dad and Grandpa sipping coffee and eating donuts.

"Morning," Mom says with a smile.

Dad and Grandpa both offer me a head nod.

"So?" I ask.

Dad turns to Grandpa Lou and they exchange a look of agreement.

"Have a seat, Jake." Dad pulls out the chair next to him and offers me a donut.

I nibble on it and wait.

"We've made a decision," Dad says. He stands and fills his coffee cup. He adds some cream and sugar then returns to the table.

The waiting is becoming too much. Don't they know what they're doing to me?

"There are two things we need to talk about," Dad says. "The first is your consequence for selling your stuff and not being honest."

I guess I'd forgotten about that. My mind had been so focused on the coin, that I figured those other issues would slide into the past and never be mentioned again.

I guess I thought wrong.

Mom sets down her cup. "We forgive you for what you did, but you need to learn your lesson." Her tone is firm. "We'll pay some bills with the $382 you earned but you'll be working off the remaining value of the stuff you sold."

My shaky leg starts and a piece of donut gets stuck in my throat. I pound my chest to get it down. "What does that mean?"

"We'll figure it out," Grandpa says. "I have plenty of raking, sweeping and cleaning to do. And it can always be done more than once." He gives me a stern smile.

My leg settles a bit as I come to a level of acceptance. I should have known that I couldn't sell everything without dealing with the fallout. Actions always have consequences. I guess I learned that in the school bathroom when Max almost drove my face into the wall. And when I had to apologize to Ben for not trusting him.

But things could be worse.

I look up and say a silent, "Thank you," to God that my face is in one piece, that Ben is still my friend and that my consequence isn't as bad as it could have been.

"Now let's talk about that coin," Dad says, interrupting my quiet prayer.

Alex walks into the kitchen just as Dad mentions

the penny. He plops down in a chair and stuffs a donut hole in his mouth. "Was goin on?" he mumbles.

I shush him and look to Dad, motioning for him to keep talking.

"We've decided to let you keep the coin."

My mind doesn't register what this means. "Keep the coin? Or keep the money?"

Dad sets a hand on my arm. "You didn't let me finish." He looks at Mom and she nods. "The coin is yours and the money is yours, if you want it."

I jump up from the table, almost causing all the coffee to jostle out of their cups. "$8,500 is mine? What about the car, and the house, and the bills and …"

Grandpa takes hold of my shoulders and looks me in the eye. "The coin will stay in my safe until you're ready for college. Then you can decide what you want to do with it."

Mom and Dad nod in agreement. "We need to trust God, Jake. He'll take care of us. Dad will get a job, I know he will," Mom says and squeezes Dad's hand.

Everyone in my family watches me as I take in

what Mom has just said. I sit and consider all that's happened. The coin is in the middle of the table, acting as a symbol of the lessons I've learned.

I rub the penny in my palm and whisper one last prayer, "Thank you God that the real thing is always better than a fake."

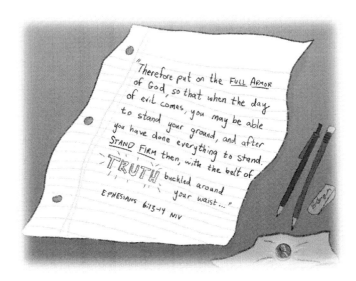

Dear Reader:

I hope you enjoyed Jake's latest adventure. Trusting God to take care of the big problems in life can be hard. But it's a lesson well learned by Jake. My prayer is that you too can learn to trust him in the big things and the little things in life.

Be on the lookout for the next book in the Coin Chronicles Series:

The Quarter Question.

And if you haven't yet read Book 1, *The Nickel Nuisance*, make sure you pick up a copy.

Finally, if you've enjoyed reading this book, please leave me a review on Amazon.com.

May God bless and keep you until next time,

Veola Vazquez

Acknowledgements

My first "thank you" goes to my husband for putting up with the hours upon hours I spent writing. Thank you for supporting my dream to write, publish and create. I love you.

To my boys who bring humor and fun into my life, I love you both. You are my inspiration. Both your antics and your words give me constant ingredients to add to this recipe I call fiction.

I want to thank all the writers and readers who have helped make this book what it is. My fellow critique group members, you are invaluable.

Finally, I want to thank Lauren Boebinger Lewis who has spent hours creating, revising and developing the images for *The Penny Predicament* and *The Nickel Nuisance*. You have made my stories come to life. Our partnership has been amazing. Thank you!

ABOUT THE AUTHOR

Veola Vazquez is a doctor, but not the kind who checks your ears. She's a psychologist, a doctor who talks to kids about their problems. She loves to read, boogie board in the Southern California surf, and take walks with her husband, two sons and two wiener dogs,

Paco & Bruce.

She loves to speak to moms and kids, so if you know someone who is interested in hearing what Dr. Vazquez has to say, visit her website: veolavazquez.com for more on how to contact her.

ABOUT THE ILLUSTRATOR

Lauren Boebinger Lewis is a Graphic Designer and Illustrator who loves to design and create beautiful things. She enjoys spending time with her husband and daughter and lives in California. Visit her website here: laurenlewis.dunked.com or follow her Bible verse artwork on Instagram: @hisword_typographicverses.

63500517R00141

Made in the USA
Lexington, KY
09 May 2017